Captain Bodacious

by

D.L. Barnes

Coastal Saga Series
Book 3

Published by Ocean Time Publishing LLC Publishing LLC.

3760 Sixes Road, Ste 126-114

Canton, Georgia 30114

Cover and interior artwork by Canva

Hardcover ISBN: 9798218222239

Paperback ISBN: 9798218225919

Library of Congress Number: 2023940273

This story is a work of fiction. The names, characters, places, and events are productions of the author's imagination or are used fictitiously. Any resemblance to actual persons, living or dead, business establishments, or locales is coincidental.

Chapter 1

THE FIRST STIRRINGS of the film crew were noted around 6:30 in the morning. Preparations for filming the scenes of the aquatic sanctuary zone two miles under the ocean surface off the coast of Georgia were underway. Few people knew about this underwater haven for sea life unless one was a diver, oceanographer, commercial angler, treasure hunter, or smuggler. Several of the team members had already arrived for the day's assignment.

The filming of the dive would happen later in the day. Some crew had already wandered to one of the three, awaiting them at the marina. The vessels would be stocked and prepared for the logistical travel of carrying the team of a diverse group of trained individuals and one non-human subterrane robot named "ZEB" to the location.

Twenty miles away was a lone man jogging along a trail that paralleled the coastline. For Matt Fitz, the best part of the morning was watching the sun rise in the east. The ball of fiery light slowly lifting from the optical illusion of a straight horizontal line reminded him of the days when ships roamed the seas. How adventurous the ancient people must have been to have traveled from one continent to the other, watching the sun, moon, and stars guide their way. He was lucky to have parents who lived on one of the developed islands off the coast of Georgia, so he spent many years running on this trail. He never tired of seeing the variation of color on the water's surface, depending on the time of the year. Sometimes he would be rewarded further by catching sight of a dolphin swimming above and below the water just beyond the shoreline. Matt brought his emotions here on the jogging path. The beach was his safe zone, where he could let down the veil of his loneliness, despair, and anxieties.

Matt Fitz fits into the professional diver category. His 6-foot frame, sealed in a wet suit and ladened with underwater gear, would be filmed during the day's shootings. Matt knew many of the crew from other projects, though he lived on the other side of the state line. He frequently did dives along the Georgia and South Carolina coast. He considered this area in his backyard.

Six hours later, the filming had been underway for some time. Matt was being directed to prepare to ascend as a part of the first team of divers to go under the water's surface and explore the sanctuary's natural habitat for sea life.

"It's time to go up." All three divers had heard the call and made the hand signal to confirm. The three members of the diving crew were ready to make the ascent. Visibility on the ocean floor was superior today. The sanctuary was teaming with the ocean vegetation and aquatic life that few ever get to experience in person.

The footage filmed during the dive was stunning, according to the camera operator filming the divers as they swam along the ocean's wonders. Clear, hot, and sunny on the topside contrasted with the cool and vibrant colors under the surface where the aquatic world lives.

Matt's thoughts were that *those who don't believe there is a divine maker have never seen the neon blue and white striped fish passing by or the orange-colored flora that lives far below the water's surface.* The goal was to film the vibrant sea life along the Georgia shores. *So far, the ocean has put on a dazzling show*, in Matt's opinion. Pirate ships and Spanish galleon wreckages maybe the conquest of treasures seekers. For Matt, the prize was seeing the natural kaleidoscope of various life forms in the world under the water's surface. He enjoyed the dive immensely. It was an inspirational activity for him. It allowed him to separate himself from his memories and previous pressures and duties in the military. Matt had been a highly trained special operations commander. As a result, he had the skills to dive, rescue, and search. On this day, he reaped the rewards of all that training, putting it towards a more pleasurable endeavor. Ascending to the water's surface, along with the other divers, Matt reentered the world of blue skies overhead. He was leaving the world of a watery paradise below. In a short period, they would be on board the research vessel.

Casey and Brad were a husband-and-wife team who were part of the diving team. They were both part filmmakers and researchers on staff with the marine biology department at the local university.

Matt and Brad had been friends since they attended the academy together.

Brad was all smiles as he talked about the footage. "I think we nailed it today!" The colors were spectacular, and the visibility was superb! I couldn't have filmed more exciting footage in the Florida Keys. Everything was like a scene from a perfectly written script, especially the dolphin shots. Those were amazing. The images looked like they were talking to Matt and Cassie. I can't wait to get into the editing room with this. The video package we present will thrill the foundation. The stills themselves are going to a worth their investment.

"That's good," Matt responded. "Just call me when my award for best actor with fins comes in. I promise to clean up and thank you in my acceptance speech."

"Oh, you are such a ham, Matt!" Cassie teased.

"I was thinking of a crusty crustacean, but ham's pretty good, too," Matt laughed. "We couldn't have asked for a better day."

"That is a fact! I'm going to upload the file for backup from both cameras and I'll be right back. I loved working from a boat like this with all the research and whistles on board. It makes my life a lot easier. Usually, I'm trying to finagle all my gear on a rubber raft or canoe in some remote area. One wrong move, and I would be steak tartare for a shark or an Amazonia snake."

While the crew awaited Brad's return, they laughed at the banter between team members. Matt was not short on stories and added a couple of his own. But the ones he didn't share were the stories that haunted him the most. Those were the ones Matt couldn't shake. He visualized putting those ghastly memories in an urn and letting them flow far out to sea. But unfortunately, they kept washing up on the shore unexpectedly. Matt tried hard to release the grief, but the pain had engulfed him for months since the explosion had happened. Trying to respect the grieving process and move on was complicated.

"I will head straight back when we dock up at the marina. I have a perspective new client tomorrow, and I need to do more research about the company. Unfortunately, I didn't have much time this week. I had a great time with you today, though! Invite me any time for one of your projects."

"You bet, Matt. Stay in touch, and let us know how to reach you. We don't like it when we can't call on you for a game of tennis or a barbeque!" Brad said.

Cassie chimed in with a warm smile. "Bring a friend! We love having you visit us!"

"Thank you. I will." Matt said.

Later that night, Matt returned home and glanced at the week's agenda. He sat and reviewed some materials sent to him and some other items his assistant had gathered for him. Tomorrow was a golf game with a mutual friend and a possible new Drew Taylor. He was the new is CEO company with headquarters now in Savannah that designed in the past had manufactured large construction equipment. The new CEO had plans to develop a line of specialized equipment and technology that met the needs of working in ocean and coastal areas worldwide. It was a pretty big endeavor, but then again, he knew the repetition of Drew Taylor, and he knew this was a champion in life. Matt was looking forward to meeting him. He thought it was a good fit for the firm, and he was the proper counsel to be the liaison. Working with Mr. Taylor felt like an important partnership.

Matt looked at the rest of the week's calendar. His assistant had filled the week with the typical tasks on his weekly schedule. However, he had a large block of time cut out of his day this week. It was an interview with A. Van Dorn. Matt recalled this add-on. He had asked his assistant to arrange his schedule so that he could meet up with Mr. Van Dorn's daughter. The man was an acquaintance of his father and an instructor of Matt's at the academy. He had a daughter a few years younger than Matt. She had moved to Charleston to work on her graduate degree, her father stated in the email. Matt remembered his old instructor and liked him immensely. He and Matt's father had stayed in touch since the days when both were instructors at the academy. *The world was small*, Matt thought after speaking with Mr. Hill a few weeks back. They discussed the opportunity for Matt to meet Mr. Hill's daughter. Angie Van Dorn needed an article for the school's magazine. Matt might have something related to historical artifacts and Charleston that she could use in the magazine. He told his assistant to make a long block of time during lunch next week. Matt planned to invite her to one of the local eateries, to have her enjoy the culture in the small coastal village. Matt would treat Miss Van Dorn with a little southern ambiance by the sea at one of the great little kitchens in town as a courtesy to her family. Then, he would give her a press release that he typically had on hand and send her away. It would be a quick afternoon, and then he would return to other things gritty and salty.

Eventually, Matt pushed everything aside, realizing the hour. It was time to pull the hatch for the evening. Tomorrow felt like it would be a wonderful day.

Chapter 2

ANGIE VAN DORN was on her way to her dream location. Having been accepted into the master's program at South Carolina College created an opportunity to be independent. She quickly alerted her parents that she was ready to move from under her parents' protective wings. Angie would seek her purpose in life away from her preppy friends, loafers, and crew neck sweaters that had been her wardrobe staple. Angie was excited about moving away from the comforts of her family, who had lived in upstate New York. Studying historical preservation was her passion. There were few better places to get firsthand experience than Charleston.

After moving into an older but cozy apartment that had been a renovated carriage house on the peninsula in Charleston's historical area, she set her goal of finding a group of friends to help her acclimate to her new surroundings. Lauren was one of those friends she had made early on. She met her one day while hanging out at the offices of the college magazine where Angie was working a part-time job as a contributing editor. She liked Lauren's fun, free spirited personality immediately. Lauren worked for the public relations department of the college. Angie remembered her first impression. True to her southern twang, Lauren was the perfect stereotype. Her genuine self is in pearls, T-shirt, jeans and four-inch heels. She was the human replica of a magnolia blossom, giant in personality and bursting with flirtatious femininity. Her nails glistened with pink polish, precisely applied, and coordinated with the lipstick. She had coifed her hair into a messy bun, pulled to perfection, allowing spirals of strands to frame her face. Lauren came in and lit the room with a bubbly burst of energy and had everyone's attention.

Angie recalled her first day at work with her mother after that first day on the job. She had gone to the office with black ankle pants, pumps, and a white blouse. In contrast to Lauren, Angie related to her mother how she had on minimal makeup, with only a smidgen of rouge and a neutral gloss to cover her lips. The bobbed haircut. Angie had worn it since the sixth grade was not working in the land of humidity and waves, she expressed to her mother. Angie's summary of her first day was that she was sure the footwear would need to be changed immediately. After the second week, Angie also added to her list of tasks was making an appointment to a salon specializing in pageant consultations.

"Angie, why don't you come over tomorrow, and you can help me get out of this funk that I'm in? I promise not to bore you with paint samples and swatches. You have such a skilled eye for design, though, and I love hearing your ideas as I'm redoing this place."

"Sorry, Lauren, I planned to interview someone for the magazine tomorrow. He lives south of here in one of those small towns on the coast near the state line. I did some research. It could be an enjoyable day trip. Jerome had this idea, and what do you know, but my father had a connection. I made an appointment with this guy. I guess he has a law degree/MBA from the College. He has been involved in projects with the museum here, too."

"Oh, that sounds interesting. What's the guy's name?"

"His name is Matthew Fitz, an attorney related to the story. According to my father, I thought I would work around the theme of shipwrecks in the area, and Mr. Fitz would be an interesting resource. I've never met him. I've spoken to his secretary, and he has emailed me about the meeting. He could be dull or obnoxious. I don't know. If Dad helped to set this up, I guess he's pretty safe to meet."

"Do you think your father is trying to be a matchmaker?" Lauren asked.

"Lord, I hope not. All his friends are stuffy men. However, my parents have been pressuring me to settle down and start the next generation, so the family line doesn't end with me. That's a lot of pressure for an only child. I was fine. Being spoiled by my parents was perfectly acceptable to me. So why would I want to share?"

Angie giggled. "They're getting more nervous after I broke off seeing Dan. My parents think I'm wallowing too long. Maybe it was that I didn't like Dan that much. Now that I'm down here, they can't track my comings and goings. I think it makes them nervous."

"They're only parents. You can't fault them for that," Lauren commented.

"Yeah, I know. I love my mom and dad, and I do miss not being around them and my favorite haunts. I have cool parents."

"So, back to this attorney. Your father has hooked you up to meet. What's his story?"

"I don't know his story. That's why I am going to meet him tomorrow for an interview. He seems like a nice guy, from what I can tell. He also appears to be busy. It was hard to pick a date that would work for us both. Given that my schedule is free, all his appointments must have taken me over three weeks to schedule this."

Lauren became more interested in the change of topic from her mood of gray. "Is he single? If so, find out what the guy likes. Does he like natural blonds vs. highly beachy blond types? Maybe he prefers curves vs. tall, athletic looks. I always thought magazines highly overrated the fragile babydoll look, although it was popular back in the sixties, not so much now. So, before you throw him back at sea, let's learn more about him. I'm not as fussy as you, and I like stuffy men." Lauren looked at Angie with a smile.

"You are a mess, but you got a deal. I thought you were dating Jarl?"

"Sometimes we go out and do things together, but he's slow about making any series moves." Lauren frowned. "Maybe he doesn't like me that much."

Angie shook her head. "Yeah, after a couple of weeks, you'd think he would have at least bought you something shiny."

Lauren responded, "Hey, I still believe in love at first sight. However, Jarl bought me a new shiny laptop on Saturday when we were out. I think he was tired of mine crashing when I was trying to do virtual meetings with him. I suspect he felt it was cheaper than driving off the island whenever I called and said I wanted to show him something on a project on which I was working."

Angie laughed in merriment. "Anyway, I got to run. I need to finish some things before I call it a night. Call me if you are still in a funk this weekend, and we'll get together. I'm dying to see how that built-in bookcase turned out under the stairs.?"

"Sure thing. Have a safe trip tomorrow. Bye."

Angie put the phone down and took her coffee mug to a chair beside the sliding doors. She opened the doors and listened for the clamor of the streets beyond the fenced-in courtyard. Occasionally, she would hear the horn of a departing ship down the floating corridor and out to sea.

Angie's mind floated back to a different era when ships took sail and traveled the globe. Angie was aware of the history of the underbelly of cities and towns that scary stories along the wharves and docks of centuries gone by. The Van Dorns had developed their shipbuilding skills in their beloved homeland before taking their chances in the British colonies in the early 1700s. Starting all over, Silas Van Dorn and his strapping three sons built a company that built elite schooners and sloops. The vessels were desired for speed and maneuverability. The smaller mast boats were faster and could transport mail and cargo along the coast's shallow inlets and upriver to where supplies were needed. Over time, the demands for such boats faded, and her ancestors moved their skills to other industries. Angie's family descended from the youngest son, Jan Van Dorn, who had two daughters, Katherine, and Kitty. Both daughters had links to Charleston during the Revolutionary war.

Angie listened to the horn of a departing ship in the river near the modern docks along the river. She tried to understand the ancestor's reasons for leaving their beloved homeland. *There must have been a light to have drawn them across the vast unknown.*

Chapter 3

ANGIE TOOK OFF for her destination about ninety miles south of her starting point the following day. Taking the old route closer to the Atlantic, Angie could take the scenic route through marshes and intercostal waterways. It was a sensory pleasure compared to the route on the interstate. She had prepared herself for the interview. Working for the college magazine came naturally to her. She guessed it was in her blood, as both parents had worked in some capacity in advertising in New York City early in their careers. Her father understood the numbers and the marketing. Her mother understood the art.

Following her GPS, Angie could easily find the address she was targeting. The small town of Sunrise was near the state line between South Carolina and Georgia. It sat along a bluff. It was a beautiful small hamlet that comprised the six blocks of the historic district and the newer homes that filling the circumference of the town. Historically, hurricanes did not make direct hits in this area because of a freak geographical feature of the continent. Angie appreciated the beautiful, canopied trees and thick vegetation surrounding the small town's outer boundaries. She could see the river flowing down on one side of the city, opening wide into the Atlantic beyond. Angie also spotted a lighthouse in the distance. Eventually, Angie looked around and saw the street she was looking for off the town's main road. It was a mix of offices and small commercial shops on a cobblestone. A small parking lot at the rear of the building matched the address on the email.

Angie thought, this building looks like the spot. She touched the banister of the old mansion now housing the offices of Spangler and Fitz. The office she sought was a typical old south charmer, the kind one thinks of when envisioning an old southern port city. It could have easily fit into the grand streets of New Orleans or Mobile port cities. One could imagine the cobbled ballasts paving the avenue for three blocks marked with footprints of saints and sinners of long ago. Angie looked around and thought. *The images still lurked as ghosts whispering along the magnolia tree-lined streets and behind the glass of second-story parlor windows.* She removed her shades as she reached the shaded sidewalk approaching the front door. Angie saw the early blooming pops of spring colors in the front yard and smelled the clean, salty air. She wanted to pinch herself to make sure she was in the moment. *She wasn't on the eighty-fourth street, and this wasn't the landmark that housed pyramids and bones of prehistoric animals.*

Angie pressed towards her assignment, turning the knob, and letting herself into the entrance. A receptionist sitting in the room on the right warmly greeted her.

"May I help you?" The receptionist's smooth, refined dialect was audible in the woman's voice.

"Yes, I have an appointment with Matthew Fitz at 11:00 today. My name is Angie Van Dorn.

"Miss Van Dorn, I will let Mr. Fitz know you are here. He is expecting you. Please have a seat.

Angie turned around and saw several wing-backed chairs of mixed fabrics that blended with the theme of creams and blues with accents of green and cranberry. She sat on the chair with the best view of the window scene outside. This quieter street off the primary thoroughfare had a more tranquil feeling. People were walking dogs and jogging along the avenue under the canopy of Spanish moss. Many of the lots surrounding the office had large sago palms absorbing the direct sunlight. The landscape designer had planted large broad-leaf hostas in the shade. The office staff had neatly stacked magazines on the coffee table, with a general theme of the local area. Angie was already picking up the vibe that this may have been a mistake. This office reeked of pretentiousness. Angie's experience told her that her demeanor of simple and straight clashed in the middle of the magnolia country. In six months, she believed those who devoured grits with cheese and eggs rather than a bowl of maple-swirled coated cooked oats were simply alien. Well, at least that was her experience with the last encounter with a particular professor of molecular biology. He was her previous official last date before leaving New York. Angie recalled *his roots had been in a small town south of the Virginia border and above the Florida line. She was leaving Florida out of the mix because everyone knew Florida was sunnier.*

Angie settled in one of the Chintz-covered chairs and settled in to read her messages. Then, after a few brief minutes, she heard footsteps behind her. She looked up to acknowledge the man before her and held his hand out to greet her.

"I am Matthew Fitz," the man said. "I am pleased to meet you, Ms. Van Dorn. Your father and I have known each other for several years now. I spoke with him a couple of weeks back. He said that you are attending college in Charleston. Lovely town."

"Yes, I am working on my master's in historic preservation. But I also hope my father mentioned I wanted to write a story about you for one of the college's publications."

"Yes, he said something about that, but I am far too dull to write about when there are so many more people that others would like to read about. We'll get to me later. You are interested in working with one of the insurance firms covering historical buildings. That could be fascinating work, especially if you like to travel. I may have some contacts for you, but let's discuss that over lunch. From here on out, call me Matt. I've cleared the next few hours, and there is a lovely spot just down the street with tables outside if we get there early enough. I'm dying to have an omelet with some cheese grits."

Immediately, Angie's hand pulled out of his handshake with a quick burst. Another male figure wearing a bow tie, much like the one in front of her, entered her thoughts. She had a dislike for bow ties that were not black satin. The interview was not starting well.

Mr. Fitz's smile became even brighter, and a twinkle in his eye showed laugh lines underneath the brows. "I'm just kidding. I can't abide grits. But take me out for some grouper and fries, and I will steal a couple off your plate when you are not looking." Matthew gestured for her to rise and walk him back to his office.

Angie's reserve had lifted momentarily, and she felt the warmth return to her cheeks. "I would like that."

As they entered Matt's office, Angie quickly peeked around the room. "It would appear that my father has been telling you some of my secrets." She smiled back, trying to be cordial.

"Only with the best intentions," Matt responded.

Angie let her guard down just a little more. There was a bouquet of things to look at in this man's office, and she was trying to pick out the most significant things she wanted to remember for the article. "This is an interesting piece of artwork you have. It looks original. Is it?"

"Most of the things over there are. They are family pieces I eventually inherited as the only male grandchild of a long line of folks that kept bits of the family's history. My grandparents left me with the family's nautical pieces. Legend has it that my grandfather, from several generations back, supported the colonists against the

British. Supposedly, he secretly transported important documents and people from the north to ports in the south. That's a painting of him when he was a young man." He stared at Angie's face. "A famous painter did not paint it. Oral tradition says his sweetheart painted it."

"He looks rather bodacious!"

Angie thought she saw a blush underneath Fitz's gently tanned skin. Quickly, she changed topics.

"Your family history is very interesting. Has that affected what you do now as an attorney?"

"Oh, that. It's just a shingle outside for me. Yes, I have passed the bar and work with Maritime law, but I'm not a trial lawyer. My name is not on the marque outside as I'm not a lead partner in the firm here. A consulting partner probably fits my title better. I have some duties that I conduct, and I have clients. I have a great relationship with the team, and it works well for all of us."

Angie turned the conversation to the painting. "I would like to know more about your ancestor in the painting." She tried to look about, but her gaze didn't want to leave the face of her interviewee. "Well, we will see. It makes most people want to yawn when I talk about what I know. Now let me get my keys here, and we'll go out. Your father mentioned that you'd been here only six months, so there's a lot to get acquainted with. Let's talk more at lunch."

Angie agreed. *What was Matt's connection with her father? She would save that question for an icebreaker during the meal.*

Lunch was fun, Angie thought, and not what she expected. They had traveled by car down the street and closer to the wharf. A narrow lane led to a small eatery with an open sitting area on the back patio overlooking the waterway. It felt cozier, with plants in urns scattered about and a colorful canopy overhead. The air blew through the protected area, providing a fresh puff of air to the cheeks and a sweet fragrance of flowers wafting in from the shrubbery and baskets on the front street. She had read a story once that said the sailors could smell the flowers in the distance as they came closer to land from the gardens as they got closer to the islands. Angie smelled a similar sensory delight. The atmosphere was like a drug.

Angie's mind went to a serious thought for a moment. *There are often periods filled with darkness. Bring beauty as an ointment to those in need, and it can lead one's way out of the gloom. She wasn't sure where the deep thought came from, but she was sure it was truth seeking its way out of her heart.*

Matt saw Angie's faraway look and did not want to intrude on her thoughts. He sipped his iced tea and took another bite of the hushpuppy on his plate. He savored the bite, scooped up and cornmeal fried delicacy with a couple of sweet potato fries, and placed them on Angie's plate. When she looked down at her plate and tried to resist, Matt touched his lips to quiet her rejection. "Enjoy it as part of being of the local culture."

Angie smiled back and looked around. She pondered, took the hushpuppy in her mouth, and enjoyed tasting the morsel's mix of seasonings and textures. *Then* Angie returned to her beet salad with slices of blood oranges, cranberries, and roasted walnuts with goat cheese tossed in a champagne vinaigrette. She blurted out "heavenly" with the first bite. Her cheeks became rosy as she felt the heat of embarrassment of showing private pleasures like this to a stranger.

Matt grinned and continued munching on his grouper po'boy. "I am an Irish potato kind of guy every day, but Thanksgiving, when I like all the fuss over my sweet potatoes. I hardly eat yams for the rest of the year. He tapped one and put a slice in his mouth."

Angie laughed. The interview was becoming a fascinating day away from the routine of work and classes.

The conversation was interesting on a variety of topics. Patrons came by the table to chat. Unfortunately, she instead lost sight of the purpose of the interview for the magazine and became more intrigued by the person known as Matthew Fitz. He moved in circles that were wider than the law form.

"Do you know everyone in town?" Angie asked after the last man with a t-shirt and shorts stopped by to give Matt the morning weather on the sea twenty miles out.

"I confess I know the right people who know the real gossip in town. That's the stuff that counts, right?" Matt smiled again with his bright white teeth. "It's a small town. We have tourists who come through, but not in vast amounts, like other towns on the coast. The larger towns have more of everything. The folks who live here don't mind having less if that means as long as they still have a sense of peaceful community way of life. You can see there are only a few hotels here. We enjoy sharing the latest catch of the day and boutique shops for the ladies. The commercialism and hype of the beaches are less attractive to many of us who live here. Should it change, I might have to pick up the sail and find another haven."

"That sounds more like living in a fairytale. It that what you like about being here."

Matt looked somewhat serious for a moment. "Angie, my work can sometimes take me to places I don't want to be and deal with things I don't see, but it's my job. The sea and sunrise soothe my nerves and make me sane in a world I do not quite understand. I do not apologize for my lifestyle. It fits me."

Angie sensed his seriousness and knew not to walk on that path today. She was not sure she ever wanted to open that keg. "Yes, well, maybe we should discuss why I am here." Angie said rather coolly, as she did not know how to pitch the banter back after his revelation. An hour and a half later, Angie looked at her watch and showed a bit of a frown. "Time passes quickly, and I hate to take up your entire afternoon. I've barely scratched the story about you and your connection with the civil war artifact you helped to discover in the harbor."

"Ah, so that is the angle for the story. Well, that wasn't a big deal. I helped some friends document where it was and what might help raise a boat. So, they get the credit for this one. I was just a first mate, you might say."

"Do you have diving experience?" Angie asked as she followed Matt's lead away from the table.

"I am a certified diver. I spent a lot of time training off the coast of Florida and the gulf."

"That's interesting." Angie replied.

Matt shrugged his shoulders rather boyishly. "I have lots of different interests. I tried to keep my skills useful for some purpose."

"Yes, I'm kind of like that, too. I make hard-tack candy at Christmas and knit toboggans in winter. Having a variety of skills is very important to me. I'm sure I will need both skills while I live here," she said with laughter. "I also have learned old English and French and practice my translating skills every chance. Ancient Gaelic is my next challenge. Opportunities to speak Gaelic are few, but sometimes I've gotten asked to work on special projects because I have these skills."

"Yes, I can see how that would make you unique and useful." Matt momentarily looked into Angie's eyes, and both parties felt the intensity. He was sure of it. "Well, if it's a story you need for the magazine, I will send you some notes on my work about the project and maybe some pictures that are part of my collection. Also, there are probably some people at the museum you could interview to collaborate on what we did to explore the harbor for historical artifacts before the excavation." Matt responded with interest.

“That would be terrific. Thank you.” Angie was stunned. She had only recently known of the Fitz family from her father. “Now Matt was helping her with an article she needed to complete.” She wondered more before she slid into the car seat of Matt’s car. “How did my parents know your family?”

Matt was quiet for a moment. “Connections between our families have been present for a long time. I know my father knew your father when they were young men. It may have been when my dad was an instructor at the academy. Yours was, too, I believe.” Angie raised her eyebrows and agreed.

Matt added. “Perhaps they drank from the same taverns I used to go to when I was there.”

“I’m afraid not. My father doesn’t drink anything stronger than a root beer.”

“Then it can’t be from my old hangouts. But, perhaps, they met on vacation or in the military. Your dad must have a lot of fun on the winetasting tours in France and Italy,” Matt said.

“You’re being sarcastic now. You know how our parents know each other because you do not lie well, Mr. Fitz.”

“Well, that’s not quite true. I can’t tell a lie to a pretty lady who needs to know the truth. All I will say is that your family has known about my family for a long time. There was a generation we may have been enemies.”

“What is it, you know, Mr. Fitz? I think your dad and my dad knew each other when we were living in New York.”

"Since this is negatively affecting pleasant our lunch, I will say that their meeting may have occurred in New York. They may have stayed in touch and traded stories over the years if they were at the academy simultaneously. But, of course, that's been several years back. There's no big mystery, and if you let me get to know you better, I might tell you more?" He smiled back and folded his hands on the table.

"Interesting," Angie said. "It's usually the women who keep up with friends and connections. You seem to know a lot more than I do."

"Perhaps their faith anchored families through the generations with a sign of hope. Those with faith often believe the right people will cross paths at the right time," Matt responded.

Angie looked at Matt. "My grandmother always said something like that when I was growing up. I'm impatient and don't like someone else controlling my fate."

"None of us do, Angie," Matt said. "It's hard sometimes not to take charge of something, especially when we want it so badly. The challenge is when something you've always wanted taken away because it wasn't the right time, person, or path. There's no real rhyme or reason. It just seems to happen."

Angie looked at Matt again, speechless this time. "You're not talking about what you learned in law school, right?"

Matt remained silent. He pushed a strand of hair that had blown across her face.

"That's better," Matt said and frowned for a moment. He imagined her hair blowing in the wind on the beach at sunrise. The darkness of her strands melting into the glow of her fair complexion hit with the rays of the rising sun and water reflections. Matt's face had a faraway look for a moment. He rebounded quickly and spoke. "No, I learned nothing in law school that taught me that. I am afraid I might need to return to the office." Matt looked up and smiled again at the young women across the table.

"Yes, of course." Angie felt the shift in the topic was a detour and accepted the turning put in the conversation.

They headed out to the parking lot and began the quick trip back. Light conversations about sailing filled the air for the next couple of blocks. That was neutral territory for them both for now.

Matt walked Angie to her car when they got back. "Angie, I will send you a file on what we discussed today by Friday."

"Thank you. That is very kind of you." She quickly pulled out her keys from her purse. "We've had a fascinating conversation today about a lot of things. I feel like I need to get back and digest it all."

"Yes, me too," Matt responded. "I would like to call you sometime and get to know you better."

Angie paused. "Yes, I would like to spend more time getting to know you better. Then maybe I will have a future assignment to work in the area, or you can come to Charleston sometime."

"That is a possibility. I'm there frequently. I also travel down the southern coast a lot, too."

"Well then, I until our paths cross in the future," Angie said from the front seat.

"Yes, I think that's likely," Matt grinned. He watched as he pulled out from the spot she had parked and walked into the building that housed his office. Before his assistant could catch his attention, Matt held up his hand, gesturing that he did not want to be disturbed for a few minutes. After a few minutes in his office, with a closed door. He emerged smiling and motioned for his assistant to proceed with her updates.

Angie returned to Charleston after her first encounter with Matthew Fitz, slightly more unnerved after meeting the man in person. She didn't remember much of the drive home. Instead, the day's past events had occupied her mind. Not until she reached the sign that showed the route to the islands off the Charleston coast did home seem like just a few miles away.

Chapter 4

AROUND NOON THE next day, a delivery van brought a package to Angie's door, along with a box of glazed pecans from a candy store from a local chocolatier. She was not feeling seduced by starting on a work assignment. She opened the note on the box from the candy store first.

Thank you for your lovely company at lunch. Perhaps a bit of sweetness will bring acceptance to a game of tennis and lunch with some friends this Saturday at a spot near you.

The gentleman keeps getting more interesting, Angie thought. She pondered the idea and opened the can. Just one glazed pecan couldn't hurt. She looked at all the whole pecans smothered in cinnamon and sugar glaze with a weary look. She closed the lid and tapped the top with her finger. Perhaps this was like when Honey tempted Samson in the Bible. She remembered most of the details, and the story didn't go well for Sam, as she recalled. Angie must have believed in something as a child. It had been a long time since she read the Bible. It seemed like as far back as high school, so why did that idea come to her head now? In fact, why was Matthew Fitz on her path at all? Few who wore plaid bow ties were ever in her thoughts of severe contenders for her attention. She didn't want to hurt the guy's feelings. However, she sought a man who reeked of adventure. *I want someone who can be silently solid and sensitive to the most delicate flower in his path.* She was looking for what was the word... *bodacious!*

Thirty minutes later, the phone blew up on the counter after showering and wearing comfortable attire.

"Hey, it's me. I've been waiting for you to call all morning. Unfortunately, I have been making miniature cheesecakes for a shower for my niece this evening. I haven't gotten free to call you and see how yesterday went."

"Well, it went. It was fascinating. Matt Fitz is a different type of guy than I usually meet, that's for sure! I'm not sure what the story is that I'm writing yet. We didn't get to my questions. But we discussed many things, and I saw some exciting stuff. He lives in a small town where everyone seems to know him. His office is in a beautiful old mansion."

"Is he young or old?" probed Lauren.

"Mr. Fitz is my age, maybe a few years older. Probably five years, if I consider, when he passed the bar. He has traits of a southern gentleman, but not those I think of when I think of an old southern boy. I don't know. He's a *mystery*. He sent me an envelope today with the information he wanted to share for the magazine. I haven't opened it yet. I've been so busy, and I was a little too nervous about opening the package. He also sent me some glazed pecans and asked me to play tennis with him and some friends on Saturday near here. I talked about being on my college tennis team. I guess he assumed that would be something I still have an interest in, which I do and would love to play, as I haven't played a game since moving here. He's playing my tune, Lauren, and he is intriguing. He makes a stranger think he is a happy-go-lucky lark. I don't believe he is, nor do the people who know him understand his authority. Where are we going with this? I just met the man, and it was for business!"

"Well, that's how things happen sometimes. Sounds good so far and might be a good match for your temperament. Are you going to take this guy up on the offer for tennis?" Lauren asked.

"Yes, no, I don't know. I haven't sent my response yet. But would it be wrong to nibble the pecans and still say no? They've been calling my name all afternoon."

"No, it's not wrong, and playing tennis sounds like a great idea. You love the game. It will be in a public place with others. It sounds like a fun way of meeting new people. I accept in a heartbeat."

"Okay, you talked me into it." Angie thought of the implications of her decision. "I just want you to know, I've been batting a thousand lately, and I don't have high hopes here either."

"Yeah, save that for the night I host your engagement party. There are a lot of frogs and a few princes, but I still like the odds if there's one tadpole in the pool which will grow up and be a prince. I'm going to find him. I am determined, strong-willed, and not easily faint of heart. I can achieve what God has given me to achieve. But, of course, I miserably fail when I run after the wrong thing. Until then, keep me up with what is happening. You have this magic of something special always happening around you. I wish I had a little of that dust around here."

"You have it. It's a unique brand, and we value having friends like you!" Angie responded.

"Thank you. Let's go shopping on Friday and help you move beyond gray, black, and navy. You're in South Carolina now. We need to spice up that cardigan."

"Oh, stop!" Angie replied.

"I mean it, six months is long enough. It's time to be one of us! But, hey, I got to go. I hear the doorbell ringing, and that's most likely the punch bowl crew. Talk to you soon!"

"Okay, bye." Angie put the phone down and looked at the can of pecans on the counter. It *seems like a good afternoon shot of endorphins to me.* She opened the can and messed with the paper packaging a little. Angie looked deeper into the box. *"Chocolate on the bottom! Oh, he's devious!" she said aloud excitedly. Angie's thoughts went flying. He knew I'd be curious enough to dig around the edges to look further before I would trust his enticement. That chocolate is war, Mr. Fitz. You better be at your best game on Saturday!*

Chapter 5

IT WAS 9:00 AM sharp on Saturday morning when Angie heard the doorbell ring and knew Matt was waiting on the other side of the door. So, with excited nervousness, she went to open the door to let him in.

"Hot coffee with a fresh bagel delivered to your door, my dear," said Matt cheerfully.

"I will take the coffee. Will you split a bagel?" Angie asked.

"Sure, I brought some cream cheese, but you must devise your recipe if you want anything different."

"Okay, I have some organic butter and blackberry preserves from the farmer's market if you would like so for your half?"

"That is tempting. I will go with a cream cheese hit and a blackberry jam slathering today. I'm feeling quiet in the mood for a killer win today."

"Fantastic! So am I, but I think simple does the trick with just some butter after toasting."

"Can't ever go wrong with the classics, Angie. So, this is your place, charming and highly sought after. So, how did you find it?"

"A professor at the college had received a grant to study in Edinburgh for 18 months. When he knew of my story of looking for a place in Charleston with a move from New York, he emailed me and asked if I was interested. I immediately took him up on his offer after he sent me some photos through email. It's fabulous, but I have only had it for 18 months, and six months have gone already. I will have to find something else the following year. It's not required of me to spend much time on campus. I could move further away and commute until I argue my thesis. Plus, I hope to be working by then in a consulting or full-time position, even if it's just in interior design, which was my bachelor's degree. I have a lot of skills I can work into something."

"That I believe. Smart girl to develop skills. That gives people opportunities in life. More people should understand that skills are essential and how one applies those skills is the key to one's potential. Let's talk about our day, shall we? I have a game arranged for 10:30 AM on a court near the home of my friends Cassie and Bradley. They have a lovely island home with dunes, waves, seagulls, and the whole shebang. In the village, we can stop and have lunch afterward. After that, it's your call. Suppose you want to come back home? That's fine. Suppose you want to see more of the island., I will be happy to play driver."

"That's an offer that sounds very nice. What would I need to wear? I bought only simple tennis shoes and a pastel tennis skirt from New York. You'll have to accept me in the stuff I used to wear in college."

Matt smiled and felt his toughness melt a little more. "That sounds fair. I like things casual on the weekends. I didn't shave this morning. It doesn't fit my Saturday routine, ever! If you were wondering, I am bathed, brushed, and expensively scented on all four counts. However, unshaved is a weekend ritual I hold on to tenaciously." He made a smile with his straight white teeth glowing. "Do the whiskers add to my appeal?" Matt teased.

His charm drew Angie into his web. She knew this guy had grown more handsome since the last time she saw him. So why did she not see it the first time they met? Perhaps she was looking for something else.

After a few minutes of chatter, Angie realized it was getting close to being on their way. I think I'm ready to go. Let me grab my stuff. I must warn you I am rusty as I haven't played in several months.

"Sounds good. I'll raise the bet," Matt bantered back.

It was a beautiful day to have a game of tennis in an ideal location. One could hear the ocean wave between points. Seagulls swooped in and out. Thankfully, the lovely white birds knew when to rise and fall to avoid colliding with a fuzzy flying ball. However, flying rackets were dangerous to anything within twenty yards of active play.

All four players took their game seriously, and no one wanted to give their partner an excuse for losing a point. Finally, after an hour and a half of play, the couples collapsed on the benches. All felt the euphoria of a fast-paced workout and were relieved that the game had finally ended.

"Next time you ask me to set up a couple's game, Matt, warn me you're bringing a ringer. That was one of the hardest games I have ever played. Wow! Where did you learn to play like that, Angie?" Matt's friend, Brad, asked.

"I've had lots of years of practice. My mother and father were talented players; we played a lot. So, I've played on clay and grass courts all over New England."

"That's the hidden secret! Did you go to college up there too?

"Yes, I had a scholarship to attend one of the private girls' schools near my parents' home. They liked me staying close. I liked it being close by too. I've been around the same friends since I was small until now. My life has been around a very protective group of family and friends."

Cassie said, "Well, honey, we've got you now and love having you. Anyone that can keep Matt on his toes for an hour and a half and not faint from exhaustion is on my team."

"Did you and Matt know each other in New York? You know he attended the military academy?"

Angie's draw dropped for a moment, and she looked at Matt with a wary eye. "No, Matt and I only met recently. He never mentioned being at the academy?" Angie looked at Matt with a masked smile.

"Yes, I was there while you were still in high school. We would not have hung out with the same circle of people. I remember many stone-faced instructors and rules, including making a bed. I have overcome all that organized rubble to have a perfectly comfortable bed with wrinkly colored sheets and no top sheet. It adds more to the laundry I perform on Sunday at 22:00 before I call it a night." He said, laughed the topic off. He was hoping the conversation didn't lead much further in that direction.

Cassie interjected again, being the grand host she was. "You two will have so much to talk about. It's always nice to run into people who have been to the same places and know the same landmarks. Let's talk about all that stuff when we pick out a place for lunch. My vote is for the grill in the village. It has excellent salads and a variety of sandwiches. I am starving and want something fast.?"

"I second that choice," Matt responded. All agreed to pack it up and pull it into the white-planked eatery at the end of the strip in the village.

Several hours later, Matt and Angie were heading back to the place. Angie's eyes were closed while she felt the late afternoon sun and the breeze from the open sunroof. This happy feeling I get from the sun and sea breezes is what I love most about being here.

It's the sunshine that makes me happy. My insides feel the warmth, and I want to float on the sea breeze. It's still so gray back in New

York this time of year- so gloomy. No wonder so many people think New Yorkers are unfriendly. It's just the gloom and the smog. They are very warm-hearted people when you get to know them. Boisterous people enjoy life even when it is gloomy. They accept the rain and move on.

"That's pretty philosophical, Angie," Matt said warmly. "I would agree.?"

"You haven't lived here all your life, have you? Though you put on the southern charm very well!"

"Well, thank you, I think. I grew up south of Savannah, where my parents have lived for years. They did not grow up in this area, though. My dad is from Illinois, and my mother is from near Knoxville, Tennessee. Her father worked with the government as a researcher. My dad met my mother through a mutual friend while studying in Knoxville. He always joked that her family made the best barbeque out of all his sweethearts, so he knew Gracie was the one. I'm sure there is a scripture related to it somewhere that will back him up. I think it was the part where the servant needed a drink of water at a well. The fairest of damsels came to offer cool water to the servant of some wealthy man on a mission. The Bible was translated to reveal that her kind heart was the clue for the servant choosing a wife for his master's son. I'm sure being beautiful didn't hurt anything. It says she was a few passages later. I'm just saying."

"Are you very religious, Matt?"

"Well, that's a serious question for a Saturday afternoon ride in the country. Why do you ask?"

"You say some things sometimes that make me think about things I used to hear in church. You seem to say them with just more- should I say 'life,' maybe? I remember my grandmother being like that. When I went to college, I just didn't get that involved. I went to vesper services and all that. My parents went to church regularly."

"We each find our path." Then, with some thought, Matt added, "It's my choice, Angie. I read the Bible and try to live by what I understand, but it's not always clear which road I should take. So, I must ask for help."

Angie looked over at Matt again. She did not feel like she wanted to pursue that topic when everything was going so nicely today. She didn't even know why she brought it up at all. "You know, Matt, you are becoming the most interesting of my acquaintances. You are making me think."

Matt smiled and followed the two-lane road back to the city.

"White egret to the left."

Angie responded as they traveled on. "They are so beautiful, like this place. It's just like another world here. It is sensual intoxication. The natural beauty leaves your senses pleasantly drugged."

Matt followed traffic down the two-lane road. Once outside the canopy of oaks, the road was wide open while the road took a bridge over the low country, and the expense of the area could be truly appreciated. "The enchanting spell of beauty is real. But I'm feeling dangerous today, so let's return to your place, and I can get you safely home. I'll let you rest after a long day. I must get back to pick up Sam at my neighbors."

"Sam? Who's Sam?" Angie wondered.

"Sam is my spoiled, shaggy canine friend who lives with me. I was told he was pure bread. Now that Sam has grown, I am highly suspicious that my canine companion is a hybrid mix that includes a bovine. He's an enormous fellow. All love him and hate no one. Well, there might be an old mail carrier he had some intense dislike for when he came around. I think it occurred after an incident involving Sam's over-exuberant greeting and a specific spray the man carried in his pouch. The mail carrier has since retired or moved away. Sam has mended his ways and only pounces on his master upon arrival. You'll get to meet him sometime, I'm sure. I want to be sure you're the right one to bring around, though, as he is the real charmer in the neighborhood. I might lose your interest in a four-legged fur ball. That would not be good for my ego or reputation."

"You sound very soft-hearted, Mr. Fitz. That's a reputation that I think you must work at very hard," Angie teased.

"Wow! You nailed me on that one. I can't hide a thing from you, can I?"

“Well, I don’t know about that, but I’m pretty good at sniffing out the truth.” Angie looked over and smiled, softening her expression as her thoughts wandered differently.

Without even a kiss goodbye, Matt brought Angie to her apartment and traveled back to his hamlet. He’d keep the secret that he was rushing home to stretch and soak after today’s vigorous round. If that was how Angie played after several months off, Matt would be glad their paths had not crossed before. Suppose he had invited her to a little fun game when she was at the top of her swing. Today, he had worn the soles of his sneakers through after the three sets.

Matt had collected Sam and walked back in the side door several hours later. He felt a warmth that had been missing for the last couple of years. Life felt sunnier, and the salty air felt more soothing today. He hoped this would be the first night he would sleep soundly in a very long time.

Chapter 6

IT HAD BEEN a few days since Angie had heard from Matt, except for one text thanking her for being his tennis partner.

"So, fill me in!" Her friend Lauren had probed when she spotted Angie at a shop in the historic district. "I don't know. I had a fun time!" Angie said across the rack of monochrome clothing. "He is very pleasant and personable when he is out of the office."

"No," Lauren said, getting her friend's attention. Lauren then moved the hangers down a rod to find a bright-colored jacket with color coordinating leggings and shorts. "This is what you need." Angie's friend tapped on a pretty tangerine and lemon-yellow print. "It's great with blue eyes. Trust me."

Angie squinched her nose a bit and continued the conversation. "He's fun to be around. And his friends are delightful. I would say he is thoughtful, but..."

"Here it comes. What's the reason for the hesitation?"

"Well, he acts like a perfect gentleman. He's become more handsome each time I see him. He's just not exciting, but he is interesting, though."

"Falling for the old bodacious fallacy, are you? That can be a dangerous path. How many nice girls run after the bad boy types, and you know how that ends?"

"Yeah, I get it. I don't know. We'll see what happens."

"Okay. I'll accept that for now. Just be careful not to lose a good one because you once found an apple with a worm in it."

"Is that in one of your latest articles?" Angie teased back.

"That was wisdom exposed from my dear Aunt Meredith, who found her true love at Slocum's grocery store in the 60s."

Angie laughed. "Should I ask if the butcher in the meat department, the right guy, was making sure all her cuts of meats were thicker than for his other customers?"

"Certainly not! The man bagged her groceries on a Friday afternoon before the July 4 holiday. He was Mr. Slocum, the owner of the chain of 10 South Carolina and Georgia stores. My aunt always teased me that the ingredients for her red velvet cake were bait. It's a handed down secret recipe."

"Do you think she used cannabis oil instead of shortening back then?" Angie teased. She couldn't help but laugh with Lauren as they continued to move around the racks.

"My lips are locked." So, will you have dinner at your house or something to get us all together? I want to check out Mr. Bowtie and see if he's worthy of my new BF.

"Maybe," Angie said.

"You will leave me in suspense, and that's okay. It gives me a reason to call you and find out the next chapter."

After selecting from the clearance rack, Angie left the discussion by escaping to the dressing room. Lauren had already purchased it when she returned and looked at some racks by the window. Angie went to the counter and made the last purchase.

"That one is going to look great on you. Let me go on now. I just saw you and had to come in and say hello! I must finish my errands to get across the bridge and pick up something before 4:00 PM. Oh well, chow, and I will talk to you soon." The young women said their goodbyes and went their separate ways.

Angie continued up the street towards the battery. And down a couple of blocks to her street. The passing horse and carriages followed her down the narrower alley where the entrance was to her apartment. Once behind the door, she walked a few more steps on the small porch that went down the long length of the house. Her apartment was on the bottom floor. Another renter had the top floor, and they had a separate entrance on the other side of the home. She seldom saw them and suspected that they were not full year residents. The courtyard was her private space, a magical spot to sit in when the stars came out. The early hours were in the morning. Then the hidden garden on the patio with the soft glow of the gaslights blended with the soft lamp lights of the living area was an oasis. One could pick out the pinks and whites of the impatient against the shaped boxwood formations, making a geometric pattern. The palms added texture and height to the garden. How different the vegetation was here than in New York. How different her life was becoming than who she was in New York. Her senses felt like she was opening and becoming more vibrant, like the azaleas in springtime.

Angie spent her Sunday evening looking through the materials that Matt had sent her regarding the article. It was like reading a press release with photos and captions that didn't require much editing except a few minor changes to fit the publication's style. She noted that there weren't a lot of pictures of him directly, but at least that was identifiable. Instead, there were photos with captions of him. Some with his underwater gear. There were photos of artifacts he had found while in the harbor during the recovery process. She had to admit that the photos were fantastic and made an interesting article, perfect for her needs. He even added consent for publication with specific restrictions. Before the evening had ended, Angie packaged the article and photos in a file and sent it to her editor. The interest was growing in who Mr. Fitz was.

Monday morning, the first thing on the schedule was class time. Awaiting was a box of envelopes containing each student's assignment. The quality of the project was half of the grade for the term. Two traditional computer-based tests determined the other half. Angie's assignment was to reconstruct a prototype of a schooner used during the colonial period. Her task was to prepare a proposal for reconstruction costs to be proposed to an insurer when total damages were inflicted after a storm.

"Where do they come up with these ideas?" she asked her friend after class.

Stanley had shrugged his shoulders. "At least yours isn't the replacement of a monument in Washington. It seems like a crazy assignment right now, but we'll figure it out."

"It's not that bad. I looked inside the packet, and Professor Bolton added some links and references to help get us started. It's just a matter of putting plausible numbers down, right? I list materials typical in construction and put them down on paper. It can't be impossible," Angie said. "It's all hypothetical, anyway. No proposal is ever exact. The professor is looking for a plausible budget and construction plan. We can do this," Angie said to her friend. "We'll just gloss it up with a nice presentation package. You are good with the graphic arts piece. I bet you can make your presentation blow the rest of us away."

"You are right, of course. You want a lift home?" Stan asked.

"No, I think I'm going to walk home today. I want to clear my head and think of some ideas for managing this assignment. The term goes by so quickly. I don't want it to slip and crash all in the end. Besides, I enjoy the sunshine and want to soak in every moment I have outside today."

"Do you think you will return to New York after being here?

"May be. I miss my family. There's no connection to keep here."

"Ah, at least not yet. I think you're going to find your purpose here, Angie."

"Yeah, maybe you're right, Stanly. I need to find my path. Let's hope it's on the beach."

"There you go, sunshine; I'll see you later."

Angie waved back and started down the steps. The temperatures had picked up the last couple of weeks. It was still comfortable to walk out of doors without feeling like one needed a shower on arrival at one's destination.

Tourists were prevalent on the peninsula all twelve months of the year. In late winter and early spring, they came in masses. Who could blame them?

"Come see the harbor and the historic district," her landlord said. "You will not want to be anywhere else."

Angie smiled to herself. Mr. Clark was right about the closeness to the historic area. Angie walked past the white-painted homes with light blue ceilings on the piazzas. The uneven sidewalks from years of tree roots growing underneath only added a unique patina to the scene. She turned a corner short of where she usually walked and traveled past a group of two homes with an elaborate, elegant feel, although smaller than some of those who viewed the harbor. A white-painted brick home tucked into a cul-de-sac caught Angie's eye. The side piazzas and courtyards burst with color now that the temperatures had remained above 55 degrees. War, fires, and earthquakes had damaged many homes over time in parts of Charleston. She suspected that these had been restoration projects at one point. She would have loved to have worked on a project that brought beauty back to where ashes had once been. Perhaps these were original and stood up bravely against the sieges of man or nature. Either way, all three homes were beautiful. Angie's mind wondered about their origins. Perhaps I will learn your story while I am here. Another block, and she would be close to her side door of the alley. She smiled at the stoop and promised to buy a potted plant at the nursery this weekend to give some color and welcome spring. Goodbye, grays. I want everyone to see the sunshine when they pass.

By morning she had rushed off for her 8:00 class. Then, she had a 15 minute to walk over to the Student Affairs building where the magazine offices were and grab a donut before sitting down with the team for the Thurs round. The meetings were casual and didn't typically last more than an hour. After that, she would meet up with George Kingsley at the museum, which she hoped would help her with information on nautical history. She also started making contacts along the east coast which would have a history of dealing with historical ship building. Luckily, her father had provided her with a list of several great contacts and offered to fly to her home if she wanted to visit any of the references in person. He would also try to review some family memorabilia and see if he could find a schooner in the files. A substantial number of documents and logs were in historical files in one college archive that he knew of from a past review of information. Matt knew he could go back and access pertinent information there.

Angie looked down at her phone mid-morning to see Matt's text.

Will you be home this afternoon for a delivery?

She texted back and responded that she planned to return at about 2:30.

Matt texted back. Perfect.

She went home by the trolley, hoping it would get to her home sooner, and opened the door at 2:35. She pulled out some water from the fridge and looked over the mail. Then, at 2:55, there was a sound at the door, and she looked out to see. There was a large hanging basket on the stoop with a card.

I've been away this week in Florida. I thought this might turn your days of gray into color. Matt.

Angie looked at the basket closer. "What a surprise!" Angie whispered and thought to herself. He is showing his charming side. She reached for and turned the envelope over to where the embossed logo and seal were. *That nursery is just over the bridge, heading out to the island. The locals knew them to have lovely things all year round. It looks like a private courier delivered it*, she thought.

The note read. *I've been away this week in Florida. I thought this might turn your days of gray into color. Matt.*

He put some thought into this. Angie took a couple more minutes to adjust the placement on the stoop to give it the best angle in the sun's direction. Once she was pleased, she gathered the card up to take the card inside and grab her phone.

Angie thought for a moment before she texted.

Thank you for the flowers! I finished your article, and it was approved by my editor today. You looked very handsome in that wet suit and tank. Angie.

A few moments later, another text came in from Matt. *I'm sure you did a bang-up job! Call me soon.* -Matt.

Angie took her phone and set it on the counter. If this was going to move into a more just an interview for a story, she wanted to slow the pace down. The mystic of Charleston. was alluring her to a walk down the street and get a coffee. Maybe she would stop at the market and buy a bottle of wine for dinner. She wanted to enjoy the adventure.

Chapter 7

MATT WAS HAPPY to be back in his home on the bluff. He needed this time to unwind and process all that was happening. The dive this weekend was successful, and Matt was sure that the company was happy with his services, though it was all business. He worked with teams that he knew and could trust. This job had to do with gathering some data boxes from a private jet that ran into some trouble before landing in Jacksonville. Since the crash site was off the Georgia coastline and within the two-mile zone, Matt had the diving documentation and the maritime law to sift. The primary goal of this dive was the black box with the critical data. The how's and the why's were questions for the experts. Matt's only role was to collect data, even if it was several miles under the sea. His experience had taught him that the unexpected could reveal unknown and lost secrets. That's why he loved what he did. The simplest of dives could bring danger. Matt wouldn't call himself fearless, but he would describe himself as determined. He tried not to allow voices to distract him from what he knew his purpose was when he accepted an assignment. Matt looked over at the lounging Sam. Pampering was Matt's parents' favorite thing to do when he and Sam were around while he was on assignment. Sam had become a celebrity when a shaggy mixed mut had shown up with his father riding in a golf cart from the house to the outdoor market at the end of the lane. "You will be hard to live with now, won't you, bud?"

Sam picked up his ears, got up to move, and sat closer to Matt. He put his furry soft snout on Matt's thigh. Matt gently patted Sam's nose and got up to stretch. "What do treasure hunters do when not looking for treasure, my friend?" Matt gathered the leather leash, and Sam ran to the screened door. "Let's prowl around, big guy, and see what's happening around town."

Matt had passed several people he knew while he was out for the walk. Finally, he stopped at the local coffee shop and ordered through the drive-through.

The owner had carried his order directly out, pulled a biscuit from the white apron, and set it down for Sam to scoop up. "Man, there you are. I thought you'd find another place to show your scraggly chin. What's up, my friend?"

"Good to see you too, Charlie! I've been south for a few days on business and added a little time to spend with my parents. My dad put me to work putting up a fence around the garden to keep the deer from messing with his garden this year. Of course, the four-legged creatures will win the battle, but it's a try."

"Oh yes. Those dear will come to the house and dig up bulbs and anything else they think is edible. So where are you down working on one of your diving trips?

"Yeah, afraid so. You've been watching the news. I received a call to assist with recovery. I didn't have to do much on this assignment. The investigators for the insurance company had moved in fast to organize what they wanted to be done."

"Ah, so when are you going to find me some treasure out there? You could donate to my early retirement fund then."

"You and me both, Charlie, Although I'm kind of there now. I like to eat, though, so I must pay the bills somehow."

"Don't we all!"

"You know, I might have seen something this time. I wanted to come back and do some research," Matt said.

"Really!"

"I don't know. Whatever I saw was only in my visual field for a flash and went away. Maybe I didn't see anything at all."

"Trust your instincts."

"Maybe. Well, I best me moving on. Sam gets impatient. He loves to scare the herons when we come down this far to the waterfront."

"Matt, you come around more. We love hearing about your adventures.

"Before I forget, I hear a real estate developer looking at the old Jones farm to develop. They're thinking of building condominiums. There's a lot of march land out that way. It will take someone who knows how to develop that kind of terrain. Who's the firm?"

"Some organization that's done some work in the Charleston area I here," Charlie answered.

"Can't keep the Shangri la to ourselves, Charlie. Got to share, be nice, and love our neighbors."

"You're right, Matt. I hate to see it get over developed and have a neon light everywhere."

"I like your neon light, Charlie. It leads me to the best coffee in town. I know what you're saying about losing natural beauty. Maybe it's a challenge for us to make better choices about how we use it. But it's time to get Sam on the road here. He must work off those table scraps my parents indulged him with during his vacation."

"Stop any time, Matt. Then I will always have a fresh part started for you."

"Thanks, man. See you later."

Matt continued his walk down to the end of Main Street, to the waterfront, and back through the side streets that led to his home.

He saw a colorful basket of spring flowers already blooming in front of one of those boutiques women like. Matt made a mental note of it. When Matt arrived at his home, he was ready to pull down the shades and call it the end of the day.

As he laid his head on the pillow, he felt his body relax. His dreams filled his head through the twilight hours. The next morning would come in just a few hours.

The next day, he was performing his routine. First, a jog with Sam at 6:00. Matt was primed for work after a shower by 7:00 and dressed by 7:30. Finally, after sending several emails and phone calls, he was ready to meet the office business. By 8:15, he was sitting at a rectangular conference table looking across the table at one of his clients, Hugh Bitters, an old army acquaintance. He didn't like the man much when he was at his command, but he felt everyone needed a chance to do something with their life. We all need help occasionally, Matt believed.

Mr. Fitz, what do you think I should do about the boat? Should I let the bank repossess it, or should it accept taking monthly losses until it's paid off? It's worthless to me, as it is after the storm.

"Let me see what I can propose to the insurance company first. I'll give them a deadline before the next installment. Maybe we have more leverage than you think. They don't want to lose a paying customer. It just looks the way it is right now because there's a lot of emotion and capital invested in that boat. So give me till tomorrow at noon to work on a proposal, and I'll send you a copy before we throw it in their court. I have the numbers to work with from the information you sent me."

"The gentleman shook hands, and Matt walked the client to the front office. Hopefully, I can negotiate something that will turn things around.

"Thanks, Matt." The gray-haired man in jeans and a T-shirt walked out the door. He owes me this, the older man said under his breath. Why he walks around like a king, and I slither around just scratching the surface, isn't fair. He spat on the ground. That's what I think of his help.

Matt looked at his phone, reading a text, before he made his next move. Finally, he typed a response and smiled.

"Is there something I can help you with today, Mr. Fitz? I noticed you don't have a break in your schedule until 5:00 PM. I could do some errands or pick up something for you?" the assistant asked.

He looked over at Kelly and gave her a big smile. "Thank you. I already have it on its way." He walked back down the corridor and went back to his office.

Kelly shrugged her shoulders. "He's been uncharacteristically happy lately," she said, hovering over the coffeepot.

"Maybe?" Mr. Spangler said.

"Do you know something I don't know?" Kelly asked.

The older gentleman pursed his lips. "No, but when I find it out, I'm not sharing. We'll consult a physician if it lingers for another five days. I'm sure there's medication for the condition." He gave her a wink. "Please interrupt at 9:20 AM with an urgent call I must take. That should break up the monotony a bit in there." Mr.

Spangler approached the conference room and opened the door, greeting the people inside.

By 5:00 PM, Matt was starving and ready to go straight home. On the way out, he grabbed a handful of mixed nuts, with Sam at his heels.

At 6:30 PM, Matt was standing inside what appeared to be an old airplane hangar. However, in this structure, boats were the focus. There were new construction and restoration projects underway. "Nestor, thank you so much for meeting me this late."

"Hey, it's okay, Matt. I've been with the staff for almost 9:00 PM for six weeks. The second shift is a better time to catch me; not as many people are around trying to grab my attention."

"That schooner is a beauty!" Matt said, admired a boat close to being finished outside in the dry dock.

"Yes, it is. I have a buyer for it already. A gentleman who lives near Wilmington flew in to see it—and made an offer on the spot. The construction with the first voyage is being filmed as a documentary for a cable network. We are doing a formal christening in the last week of March. I'll send you an invitation."

“Thanks, I’d love to come,” Matt said.

“After the christening, she sails into Charleston and enters the harbor with grandeur during the festival. I made reservations for my wife and me to be in Charleston to watch her sail into the mouth of the river before she docks at the marina. She’ll stay on exhibit for several days before making her last leg home.”

“Now, that sounds spectacular. I have reasons for being in Charleston today, so we must stay connected. Let me pick up the tab for dinner one of those nights. I know of a lovely date I would love to bring, and I see a mutual connection between your line of work and hers.”

“You are just full of surprises, aren’t you, Matt? Well, I would very much like to meet her, and yes. Yvette and I would love to join you for dinner while we are up that way. I am sending you an email to inform you of the arrangements. Back to business. Is there a boat you have picked out? It would thrill me to make you a copy of the one we’re sending to North Carolina.”

“That one is not in my budget, I’m afraid. Maybe one smaller and faster.” Matt responded.

“I think we can build you one that would be perfect.”

Matt looked around at all the activity. “What’s the one you are working on over there that looks like an old shipwreck?”

“It was. An amateur diving group found the remains south of John’s Creek in a cove buried in six feet of muck. It looked like a cannon had hit it. The dating of the wood puts it in the civil war period. It wasn't in good enough condition for the museums to want it. Sometimes the state doesn't allow these things to be removed from their resting place. The community raised private donations to excavate the wreck, and then grants were added to replicate what was missing. It was brought here as salvage. We are using it to help train students in the skills of ship restoration and building. It's a collaboration with the university and the local trade schools. It's the apprentice concept, except the students don't stay long enough to learn everything, but it can inspire a career. Once completed, they will display it at one of the local university museums representing marine research along the Georgia coast."

"Wow! That sounds like an exciting project and a winning idea for everyone." Matt said. "Before I go, can I ask a favor of you?" Matt held out an envelope. "I'm going to leave these numbers with you. I would like you to glance through the figures and see if they sound reasonable for what I am asking. You don't have to spend much time on it. I've done my job if my calculations are realistic and not out of the planet. The drawback is I need your answer by 11:00 AM."

"Sure, I can do that," Nestor said.

"Thanks," Matt responded. "By the way, do you still have connections with Bill Horton?"

"Sure. I see Bill and his partner a good bit."

"I may want to talk with them about something," Matt said.

"That sounds interesting," Nestor responded.

Matt shrugged his shoulders. "Maybe nothing. I'm going to do some research first."

"Matt, you and I know you're too busy researching anything."

Matt smiled. "Still, I need some time to check on the facts. I reported it anyway, just in case. You've had a long day. I need to let you finish. Thanks again for your help, Nestor."

"Any time Matt. I'll be in touch."

Matt returned to his vehicle and found his way to the highway leading him home. Luckily, it wasn't far. He looked at his texts and saw the one he had embarrassingly waited for since this morning.

Just ending my day. I'm glad it made you smile!-Matt.

Chapter 8

SATURDAY FINALLY ARRIVED. Angela had put on her favorite pale pink, scooped neck t-shirt accessorized with a little diamond encrusted circle on a gold chain, the one that symbolized that one was never alone. Her southern friends had educated Angela that the necklace was perfect for any attire. Angela hoped that their recommendation met oyster shucking, too. As Matt had stated, the plan for the day was hunting and preparing oysters for a low country dinner. *I'm willing to do anything once,* Angela thought when he proposed the idea the other night. Having a date with Matt was becoming much more interesting than going out for a beer and a pizza. It became more like a wild adventure, with traditional courting used as the salty ingredient to make it feel right. Angela laughed off the thought that Mr. Bodacious may be Mr. Right for a lifetime and not just for right now. It's silly to think that a man who wore a bow tie and plaid trousers at their first meeting would attract and not repel her affections.

Matt had arrived as expected with his four-pawed sidekick, Sam. After a pleasant walk along the harbor, the trio returned to the historical abode. Angie quickly picked up her day bag, and they were off. This time they were going for a day with Brad and Casey, shucking or "mucking."

Later that day, Brad described the procedure, as the sandy muck oozed between his fingers as the guys plucked the oysters and put them in the bucket. "They don't teach you the important things like this in college. It's all experience!" Brad told Angie as he loaded another bucket into the back of the truck. "If you came from New York to attend college here in Charleston. Then I think it's our responsibility to show you what is worth learning here."

Angie smiled back and looked over at Matt, whose hands were heavily covered with a smear of muck with a streak along his left cheek. She laughed. "You are so right. I would not have missed seeing Matt get his hands messy in anything!"

"You may not believe this, Angie, but I often get into messy situations. You have the benefit of seeing me in my most beautified state. Most of the time, it's like this, up to my armpits in muck!"

Cassie chimed with her soft southern dialect. "Either way, you are just as cute as a button. You can clean up when we get back!"

By 6:00 PM, the table was set on the back patio of the island home where Casey and Brad had their home. A few others came to join them at the oceanfront home at Herron Run. Entertaining with friends was like having a small group of family stumble in, each sharing their tales while keeping the lanterns burning until midnight. Even Sam had a unique role in the group with his swishing tail back and forth now and then to let the guests know that, despite the dog's drowsy pretense, he was on watch duty. Sam was prepared to pounce on the slightest movement of an unexpected intruder. Matt's canine companion was aware of his environment. Sam left no squirrel or human unnoticed.

It was the early hours of the evening when the trio that left Angie's place several hours early returned.

"Take the room in the loft. I have an air mattress up there. It can get warm, but if there is a thermostat at the top of the stairs, it can cool down quickly.? Angie put the pillow and blankets in Matt's hands. She smiled back. I'm getting up at 6:00 Am for a run. You can sleep in or join. I'll see you in the morning."

Matt took the items. "Got it, Captain. Wouldn't miss sharing the morning with you for anything else." He kissed her on the cheek. "In the morning, my angel."

Later that night, Matt was still looking through the small, rounded window in the loft area. Someone was out there and had been watching his comings and goings today. He lost their surveillance when he drove behind the gate on the island to Brad and Cassie's place. He couldn't rule out that they had not been watching by sea, as several small boats were anchored off the shoreline in the area. Whoever it was hadn't gotten close enough to alert Sam. *Who was watching my steps? What did they want to know? Matt was filtering through most assignments. I must have stumbled close to somebody's secret.*

In the morning, Angela was up as promised. Sam looked at her with eagerness as she passed the door to the alley. She leads the shaggy companion outside to a small park across the street. A few people had already started their day by walking or jogging along the city's back roads. She had planned to check back with Matt when Sam began to bark and race around her as she reached the end of the block. Not seeing anything unusual, she leads Sam back with resistance to the apartment. She looked around again and saw nothing unusual. As the city awoke, delivery trucks and people slowly drifted down streets and sidewalks. She thought nothing more and went inside.

By this time, Matt was inside, working on his computer. The stubble on his face showed he had not shaved this morning, and hair cascaded in swirls across his head with no specific direction. Yet, without regard to his appearance, he smiled when Angie and Sam returned through the entry.

Angie looked embarrassed. "I hope you don't mind, but Sam seemed eager to get outside this morning, so I took him down to the park and back."

"That's fine." Matt came closer to give Sam a rub on his head and. Give Angie a quick kiss on the forehead. "He loved it, I'm sure."

“Would you like to come running with me now? I’m ready to go again. That’s why I checked back?”

“Sure, but let’s see if I can leave Sam here. I don’t want the competition.” Matt said.

“Okay,” Angie responded.

Matt led Angie back outside, and the two began their 5-mile jog around the city streets. They stopped for coffee on the way back and slowed to a stroll at the last mile together, looking in the windows at the little shops in the historical business area. Though none were open, one could preview the shop’s windows, some filled with Charleston’s best. Paintings of the low country were displayed in several studios. Boutiques housed sleepwear designed for romantic getaways and honeymoons. A favorite of Angie’s was a cottage store with brightly colored fabrics and furnishings on display. Several jewelry stores dotted the main street with advertisements of popular settings for the diamond of her choice. Matt noted Angie’s descriptions of those things she loved the most. The painting of three sailboats on the water reminded her of a picture her father had purchased in New England. Matt’s preferred store while shopping with Angie was the lingerie store. Angie commented on favorites while her partner for the walk decided he would return solo to make a purchase when the store was open for Angie for a special occasion. *Matt was discovering feelings of having an enjoyable time with this cute and funny companion. Shopping in the early hours on a Sunday morning when the stores were closed wasn’t so bad.* Sharing coffee and conversation with a beautiful blond in a ponytail surrounded by shops, sago palms, and piazzas wasn't so bad. It was a remarkable change from his months in darkness after the death of Naya.

As they got closer to home, he sensed he had a couple of followers that had joined them several blocks back. Matt walked Angie back to her place, ensuring nothing was disturbed inside. Then he said he would take Sam for a long walk and get something out of his car after a few minutes inside. After that, Matt would take Sam for another long walk. He would be back in 10 minutes.

Angie continued her morning routine. Thinking that Matt would be right back, she showered and started looking around for something to make for breakfast. Seeing that Matt had not returned after her shower, Angie put off making a fancy omelet or French pancakes. Instead, she put a box of cereal on the counter with a bowl and the sugar pot. She figured that keeping things simple was better today than trying to corral this man with domestic bliss.

Matt returned 30 minutes later. "I'm sorry it took so long. I had to change the tire on my car. Must have driven over a nail or something," he told Angie.

"Oh, I'm sorry that happened."

"No problem, I had a spare. I just called for someone to change the tire. The mobile repair company came quickly. I might wait to take it to a tire shop this morning. I will see if it can be repaired. Otherwise, I will buy a new spare. Something will be open soon."

"I wondered when you weren't back, but that's okay. You'll miss my family's favorite breakfast today. You'll have to go with the runner-up."

He laughed sheepishly. "I'm sorry. I've got something in mind to make it up to you, but you'll have to wait until the end of the month. It's a festival and all. There's a lot going on up here, then. I don't know if I can plan perfectly, but I have my thoughts. Besides, my favorite is the green-colored circles as he pulled one from the box." He dropped a red one in her hand. "This one is for you, so you'll remember me."

"You are so smug, charming southern ...."

"Yes. That's me, a southern gentleman with a Scotsman's passion. I also have an Irishman's love for poetry and ballads, which who has a love for natural blonds, long walks on the shoreline, and sharing wit with a smart, beautiful damsel who can compete with the brightest man or women!"

"When you put it that way, I know you were out there with a sampling of some of your ancestors' best."

"Ah, that hurts when I was trying to say something lovely about this beautiful lady I have found and do not wish to leave. However, I must go for now. As I have something on which I must work."

Preparation for returning to his home was needed. Shortly afterward, Matt reluctantly said his goodbyes and started on the return track. He was watchful of those who followed and passed him on the highway. At the same time, Matt had a lot on his mind before returning home. It was difficult to be while part of his mind was still thinking of what he left behind.

Chapter 9

TWO DAYS LATER, Matt was in his office. After making a few phone calls and reading some articles and public notices, his mind spun into a likely scenario. He was attempting to work through a deductive puzzle. *What could it all possibly mean? Why would someone want me followed to Charleston and track where I was, then try to keep me there longer on Sunday so I couldn't be elsewhere.*? It didn't seem like they wanted to harm me, but they wanted to keep me away from something. He tried to rack his mind for clues. Finally, needing some fresh air, Matt left the office for a while and got some fresh air. Matt's projects weren't the work he needed to spend hours in the courtroom. Matt needed to know the law to keep his clients out of one. So, he picked up an iced tea from the local vendor and walked down to the marina. Matt didn't feel that someone was following him here, *so what about Charleston was different, or was it an important day? Somebody needed to know where he was and ensure he wasn't somewhere else on a particular day. That could be the motivation behind someone following him in Charleston.*

He later returned to the office and saw the invite for the boat christening that Nestor had been working on the last time he visited the shop. The invitation was perfect. He immediately texted Angie to see if she could clear her calendar for the weekend. Matt had some plans in mind. He glanced down at Sam and brushed the fur on his back. "Sam, my friend, I must leave you with Dad for this. He has a nicer boat, anyway."

A few minutes later, he got Angie's response, and the plans began. *What does a southern gentleman need to do to woo the heart of the women he wants to spend the rest of his life with.?* Matt would spend the next few days finding that out.

The following day, Matt was in the office. He had prepared a contract to address the relationship between the legal counsel of his firm and the Phoebe Farmer Foundation. That was straightforward. Matt could relate to the Foundation's sincere purpose, and he clicked with Drew Taylor on many levels. When a loss is so significant, there are two choices. One could curl up and die in pain or move on to build a purpose that transcends the enormity of loss. Typically, those first steps are not on one's own power. The one left needs help, they can't see. Yet, they find it's there sometimes after the journey has started. People are only the conduit for the strength in his opinion.

Matt had several other things on his plate today. He had some business in Charleston but wanted to avoid alerting Angie of his whereabouts. Matt couldn't lie to her, but she would sniff out the truth. *Maybe if he could tie it to the arrangements for the regatta, which would work. Nestor's boat was coming to Charleston harbor this weekend. That might distract her from questioning any other motive.* He needed a backup plan in case she spotted his presence while he was in the area.

Matt also looked at the information he had gathered around a potentially odd feature on his last dive. He had already put in a notice to the proper authorities about it. There had been no prior reports of any anomaly from what Matt knew. He was also unsure of what he saw. However, Matt wanted to do what he felt was prudent. He doubted if anyone had gone to take another look and thought about taking a second look himself. He could file for a permit, which is what he would do today. His curiosity was more than enough motivation to take a second look with another group of eyes. He was not a treasure hunter but enjoyed finding out about the sea's mysteries, specifically the seacoast. Pirates didn't impress him, and material treasure seekers didn't motivate him. The story of people and their decisions about life intrigued him. He wanted to hear their stories and know what they knew of the world in their lifetime. Matt laughed as he thought, *I would have loved to have been a Roman soldier in the life of Jesus or a wise man in the courts of Babylonia. Indeed, there was a yearning for God since man's first day.* Matt picked up his phone and read a text. He stood up and went for the door. *Here I go again. My mind wants to wonder about my responsibilities for today. I need to pick up the pace and follow up with my next appointment.*

Angie was happy to have someone in her life that made her happy. She had been lucky to have made a few friends since her arrival in Charleston. But, unfortunately, today was one of those adventures where her mind should be on her studies and working on the magazine assignments as part of her constant juggling of things in her life.

Angie had prepared a list of questions to find answers to in her next article. She accepted Lauren's idea of meeting her friend at the city's planning office. Several displays were present in the lobby.

"It's difficult to harness nature," Lauren said. She looked at each project presented by the planning agency and thought about where their primary areas to focus on within the next two years.

Angie and Lauren strolled around the room.

"Yes, it is," Angie said as her thoughts returned to the present. "It's hard to deny the truth."

Lauren looked over at her friend with a questioning expression. "What? Are we speaking about the same things, Angie? I think something else is rolling around up there," Lauren teased as her gaze went to the top of Angie's head.

Angie smiled. Realizing her thoughts were somewhere else. "You caught me on that one," Angie responded.

"In that case, let's change topics. What's on your mind? That appears to be much more interesting," Lauren said with a smile.

"Nothing!"

"Really?" Lauren said with her eyes going even wider.

"Lauren, I just don't know what I'm supposed to do to attract him?" She shrugged her shoulders, expressing despair.

"Honey, you have already done that, so what is that? You don't think you have to attract this handsome fellow of yours?"

"I'm not you," Angie said. She was hoping to none was in earshot. "You make it look so easy. You wear more than one-inch heels, and your nails are always perfect."

"I rarely wear nail polish, haven't gotten a professional manicure since an outing in high school, and do not have a credit card to any cosmetic stores. My department store cards do not count because I often shop for running clothes when I feel blue."

"Oh, silly, it's not all about that stuff. It can help like painting kitchen cabinets to freshen up a kitchen, but the bones must be there for someone to say that's the one I want."

"Are you saying I'm too skinny? Like what part of my body would that be?" Angie asked with jovial sarcasm.

"Angie, you are too analytical here. It's all about what's on the inside. Cliché, but true. I like my tangerine finger polish in the spring because it shows that I like colorful spring and summer flowers. They are bright and exciting, as I feel when skiing in the water. Sometimes I enjoy watching the sailboats out on the harbor with their white sails, so I put on my T-shirts and sandals to feel the breezes coming off the water while watching them. The pearls come because I like to be feminine. No big deal. I love all those things, and people who value those things come around me like a mosquito to a lightbulb."

"So, what is wrong with my picture? I like fun, and I like to be girlie, but I feel like I'm too boring?"

"That is your problem. First, you are putting too much thought into it. You are not boring at all. You are a kind person who leaves little thank-you note and remembers everyone's birthdays in the office. That's thoughtful. You are intelligent and talented. That's why you get the assignments you get. I would love to write about people in the now that are doing things that influence the world. Instead, I'm chosen for the before and after shots of garden homes in the historic district. I don't mind. I love it! They don't ask me to write about life-changing medical treatments for cancer." That always goes to Stanley. We attract things and people because we have something people want or need to draw out. For instance, my friend, Jarl, is bashful and cognitive, if you know what I mean. Jarl needs that sunshine that I bring that is light and entertaining. I can draw that out of him, and he likes that. I like his quiet inner strength most of the time. Although he annoys me when I want to go out and be seen, he wants to stay in and watch the March basketball tournament on cable. I think I will stop paying the cable bill that month. Then I won't have to spend several evenings with his attention on hairy legs in shorts running back and further for two hours. I know it's not me he's looking at because I was not fond of a day with stubble. Okay! Now you know my dirtiest secret."

Angie laughed until tears seeped around the rims of her eyes. "You are too funny, Lauren! I liked you the first time I met you because you came to my desk and offered me a hard butterscotch candy on my first day of work."

"Yeah, I remember that. It must have been close to the end of my payday. Usually, it is a small block of chocolate from the chocolatier down the street."

"You know the place too? I received a box from Matt after our first meeting. It must be a landmark," Angie replied.

Lauren showed an amused grin. "It is one of those local places people use when they want to say I like you. Do you like me?"

"Wow, that's sweet."

"Yeah, the bite sizes of bliss are. Most morsels are about six hundred calories a piece, so if you get a lot of chocolates from the same person. It probably has another meaning." Angie laughed, and her girlish dimples showed.

"He stopped after one, so we're still in the like phase."

"Great! Let's think about what your agenda is for the next few weeks. What do you have in your schedule to keep filling up your gas tank? What are you doing so you don't moon after you know who?"

When Angie got home, she was ready to take off her work clothes and grab something comfortable. She would further rewind at the breakfast bar with her computer. She could take a walk after heating the minestrone she had made the night before and shared with her editor this morning in a thermos that read, *you're the boss.* Angie would follow up with an evening walk to burn off those extra calories from lunch today. Maybe she would put on some music and enjoy some quiet time before she could so that she heard knowledge on the door. "Who would come by this evening?" She peeked through the keyhole and made out the image of prominent floppy ears. Angie immediately laughed and opened the door. "I've got to say you come with your surprises."

Matt kissed her on the cheek and put the bunny in her arms. "I couldn't resist. I've got a crate in the car, and if you don't want fluffy here, I will take it with me and find a suitable home. Sam might be jealous and all. I don't want to wake up with fur and fluff shreds through the house by the time I get home from work tomorrow. I suspect more golden fur patches rather than cotton ball puffs to sweep up after the battle of the fur balls ceased. Sam's a big lug with a larger heart. Bunny looks like a lot of fluff and puff, but I suspect she has a bigger bite than Sam's bark."

Angie laughed as she ran her fingers through the long fur. "She's so cute. Blue Dutch, just like my dad used to give me as a child at Easter. I don't have any rabbit food here. We'll have to go out and find something that Bella wants for supper?"

Matt raised his palm and stopped her in mid-sentence. "Nope, I have that taken care of, too. I bought enough rabbit supplies that should get you through the first month. After that, you can mix up your concoctions. So, do you want to keep her?" Matt asked.

"Of course I do!" Angie said as she brushed the fur on the back of the rabbit with her hand.

"That's settled. What should we call this hopping fur ball?" Matt asked.

"Belle!"

Matt looked at Angie with a grin. "Beautiful, that fits nicely. I think Belle has found a new home!"

"Let's bring her over here, and I will put a blanket down. So, what brings you uptown?"

"I had some business in the area today. So, I thought I would 1 stop by and see you before I drove back. Past this farm selling Easter bunnies, and I couldn't resist. I felt sending you a chocolate bunny from the candy store was distasteful.

Angie looked up and laughed. "Did I say something that odd?"

"No, you didn't. But you said exactly right, and Angie gave him a friendly kiss to thank him."

"Seems like I'm living right today. Have you gone out for dinner yet?

"Well, I had soup, but if you let me fix you something simple, I can make you a supersize sandwich like you might remember from Zaki's near the academy. I can plop some chips on the side. See, I have been to some of your past haunts."

"Yeah, that was one of them," Matt smiled with an almost embarrassed look. "That sounds like an excellent pub grub to me. What are you having?"

"A bite of yours, of course, and a giant pickle spear.

"You are bating me, Miss Van Dorn, and I do like a little trouble. But beware of who you are teasing. I have my paybacks. It all sounds good, though, and I'm accepting the offer. Let me get Belle's dinner and accessories from the car, and I will come and help you in the kitchen."

"Great!"

Matt went outside and looked around. Nothing seemed out of sorts today. He hadn't seen anything suspicious since his last visit when he had a flat on his car and felt like someone had been following him. He reached for several items and brought them back inside.

Three hours later, Matt woke after feeling a wet nose twitching against his chin. Since he knew this was not a soft kiss from Angie, he opened one eye and looked at Belle with piercing eyes. "You were not the female I was waking up with in my dreams." He looked around and saw that Angie had curled herself up on the floor, watching an old video of someone hiking on the Appalachian trail in Vermont.

"Angie, how long have I been sleeping?" Matt said as he awoke on the sofa.

"About an hour and a half. Not that long. I didn't want to disturb you, so I went and showered and did some things before I sat here and relaxed. You don't snore."

"That's good to know. Did I say any of my deepest confessions while I was sleeping?" Matt looked around towards his computer case. Nothing looked disturbed. He felt relief.

"No, I was listening for an old girlfriend's name or a spice story from your imagination coming through. But I saw you peacefully sleeping and didn't want to bother you."

"Ah, thank you. It seems Belle here wanted to get Frisky. Had it been you, I would have let you have your way."

Angie laughed. "I'll keep that in mind. I was watching someone hiking. That stretch of the trail I've done. It's pretty hard, but it's fun as a day trip. I wouldn't do a long-distance hike. I like showers too much."

"Me too. Why don't you come to sit beside me, so you are not on that hard floor? I will have to drive back soon, but let's spend a little time together before I go."

"Okay." Angie plopped on the sofa wearing a long jersey-like T-shirt that reached a few inches above the knee. That she often relaxed after her shower. She curled her legs up beside her and leaned into Matt. "That's nice," Matt murmured.

"Where were you stationed in the service?"

Matt knew this conversation was coming. He hoped he could be as honest as he could without recoiling into himself as he often did. "My last spot was in the middle east. I was with a team that I knew very well. Some of us had met at the academy, like the generals in the civil war. Many of us had known each other for a very long time. We knew either other's quirks or strengths. We covered each other's backs. That was our duty. I was a strong swimmer when I was young, and I learned how to be a diver when I was in the academy. I continue developing my skills, so now I use that expertise on dives or as a consultant with my law practice."

"It sounds like it could be rather dangerous work."

"It is. I try not to take on something I don't think is worth the risk. Also, I don't take on assignments that I don't think have some significant importance in material wealth. I am not critical of treasure hunters. Some of them are my best friends, but I don't have a taste for that kind of thing. I'm all in if it's for safety, gathering important information, or learning something beneficial. The other is for someone else to explore. I'm not being noble. I only use my skills for what I think was given to me, so that's my work. Are there any more questions you would like to know about me? I'm a pretty regular guy. I like pizza and beer on Sunday afternoons when football season after October. Watching the teams after they have shuffled around in the standings filters out the early stuff in the season doesn't interest me. I work a lot, but I like my fun too! One of my favorite things is to take a pretty lady to lunch during a workday because that's a pleasure."

Angie blushed. "Have you ever followed up with chocolates?"

"I did, with my evening date Jeannie Patterson once after the senior prom. My father taught me it was a friendly gesture if I liked her and wanted to go out with her again, which I did then. She was the prettiest girl in the junior class, I thought. Later that summer, she won a local beauty pageant and went on to bigger things. I received a dear Matt letter in my first year at the academy. I was following the same curse as a former cadet and later Union general who received a rejection notice from a sweet Georgia belle. He never saw her again, and neither did I."

"I'm sorry," Angie cooed as she brushed his hair away from his eye. "I hope you'll let her go," Angie teased.

Matt took a deep breath. "Jeannie has long been put away." Matt paused again. "There is someone else I need to tell you about, Angie, because it matters, and somebody will inadvertently say something. I want to tell you before that happens, so you will have insight on how to respond. I was engaged to be married before now. It was someone that I had met while I was in the military. She was an interpreter. Her name was Sela. She was with our team for most of the last year and a half that I was there. Unfortunately, she was killed when a land mine exploded as the vehicle in front of mine passed over it. Naya and three others were killed instantly. A fourth survived with some injuries. I saw the body parts; I say the bloody finger that held the ring. There wasn't a moment where I held her in my arms as she was dying, as she was already gone." Matt became emotional. "I won't share any more details, as I don't allow the memory to surface. But you need to know what happened to my heart and why it may not work as you hope or expect. My heart shattered that day. The love of my family, friends, and unexpected people has helped glue it back together, but it's no longer the perfection of a young man with his first love. I have a patched heart and a wounded soul. Perhaps I've cleaned up some of my life. I view things differently, and I know I'm not the same person I was before she died, and I never will be."

"Matt, thank you for sharing this pain. I wish I could erase it, but I hope my arms are tender enough not to cause you to carry that loss by yourself anymore. I mean that. Just feel my love right now as you remember that hurt. The tears I feel from within me can help heal; I know they can."

They both sat for some time, sharing their hearts. It was their moment in the story they were creating together.

Matt returned to sunrise a few minutes past midnight. The neighbor's son had returned Sam to his home a few hours earlier after Matt texted them about the expected arrival time. Their son enjoyed having the companion, and neither boy nor dog seemed worse for the wear. Matt always contributed to the youth's weekly allowance whenever Sam stayed over. Sam was always in good spirits on return, and the boy and his parents seemed to enjoy having the four-legged youngster around, so it worked out well.

In the morning, the sky was blue, and the sunshine was beaming down as he entered the law firm's back door. The assistant brought the documents that Matt had requested for this morning. It was back to routine. He wrapped up several loose ends before he took off for a long weekend at the end of next week. He had to make some calls and send emails so that some of his clients would not bring last-minute projects in and expect Matt to complete them in a day or two after leaving them at the office. If needed, one of the other attorneys in the firm could address the issue while he was gone. There was a dive scheduled with one of his partners. A permit had arrived yesterday while he was gone. Matt and his diving partner would explore the ocean shelf for signs of a shipwreck in the suspicious location. He had permission to photograph and describe the site for documentation purposes in order to confirm that there was a shipwreck or other historical anomaly present. It might be nothing at all.

By the end of the day, Matt drove past the staging area for the boat that Nestor and the employees had been working on. It had been pulled from the hangar and moved to the launching area along the river. She was a beauty. What a talent to build something as majestic as this replica of a 1700s schooner. Even with the sails closed, it was still a handsome form of transportation. This one was meant for a simple crew and a cabin below that one could travel up and down the coast, even in the open seas. The schooner looked like part of a brilliant ship in the water. Tomorrow, the voyage to Charleston would begin past the beaches, maritime forests, and barrier islands. How beautiful this private boat would look as it sailed past the golf courses and high-priced resorts built along the ocean front. *Would someone unexpectedly see the masted vessel as it passed the deadly point where sailors dared to tread centuries ago and dream of pirate stories?*

Matt thought it would have been a common sight at one time. But then, He looked up and saw the cylinders streaming above the clouds. The jets would someday be as unique to a sighting as three-masted schooners were today. Matt knew little about the real past and nothing about the future. He thought of his ancestor's portrait in his office. *What were the sights and sounds the sea captain experienced in his lifetime? He must have passed the point where sailors dreaded along the South Carolina coast below Charleston. The locals knew it as a sea graveyard because it was a frequent spot where ships faced the intense battering of the Atlantic. Many crews and cargo found the involuntary final departing location of their voyage at that point. The evidence of their passing showed up in shredded personal items and broken wood planks on the shore where the grand white house* stood as a gatekeeper. Those lucky enough to survive the storm and wreck were projected from the ocean onto the shoreline.

Matt's mind recalled the stories about the captain whose portrait hung in his office. Did he carry secret cargo out of Charleston Harbor beneath the noses of the British fleet for the colonists in a similar ship? Could he have been more of a pirate, as some documentation for Captain Hawke stated, or was he motivated by another cause entirely? Why did it matter? Matt waved the question away from his thoughts. The captain must have had his secrets, Matt reasoned. Just then, he heard thunder in the distance, and his mind returned to the present. It was time to go home. He had a mission that needed immediate attention, and it involved a blonde sparrow that he needed to catch before some other bad guy did.

Chapter 10

THE WEATHER IN Charleston had been perfect all week. Humid and warm was the description for the five-day forecast.

Angie had specifically arranged her schedule. As a result, she had the freedom to enjoy the festival with Matt and put in all those things that had to be turned in at school and her job. As a result, it was easy to finish the project for the marine historical preservation project, given Matt's input.

The magazine had another story coming out with her byline. It was nice to see her name in print. The topic this time was marine salvaging and coordination in Charleston harbor. Matt's contacts proved heaven-sent when Angie began her research for this article. She built a storyline angle about a family-owned, world-class company specializing in large equipment and logistic support for marine engineering projects. It was a pretty heartwarming story, even though she kept the topic focused on the company as the public relations liaison had requested. Angie was thrilled to have met the family heir, Drew Taylor, in person and learn of his coastal ties to the Charleston area. Angie's editor loved the article, and it became the cover story for the next quarterly issue. The graphics department also did an excellent job creating a haunting and exotic cover. W*ho would have thought the scrapes and dings on metal surrounding aquatic life would be so fascinating?*

Angie and her friend Lauren had gone out together on Monday to pick up some things for the weekend that Matt had planned. Would he notice her favorite fragrance she bought recently from a local French-style perfumery? Would he prefer the tried-and-true classics? They laughed when they collaboratively decided on a must-have from one of her favorite boutiques.

"That one is the bomb!" Lauren giggled when Angie held it up to show her friend. "He won't get away with that, even if he tried. I don't believe this guy is trying hard to escape, though. You better commit or let this one go for his sake because he's on the hook. He's too nice of a guy to lead him on if you don't think he's the one for you."

"I know, and I agree." Angie turned her face away. She changed the subject by requesting Lauren look at a display of pink-colored sunglasses.

By Tuesday evening, Angie could barely wait for the weekend. Matt was planning on driving north by noon on Thursday so they could drive to an island east of Charleston and watch the three-masted schooner pass by while they watched from a secluded beach. That sounded romantic, at least, *Angie thought. On her way to work, her thoughts continued to be filled with excitement. Did he have something very special planned? Or was this going to be another weekend when she wondered if he would ask, and then the most opportune time faded like vapor? Angie's imagination was pulled back to reality when Ms. Wrong side of-the-bed drives in behind her at the coffee shop and honks her horn because she was taking too long to find the lone credit card that was not maxed out. That is followed by a y sprint through the rain to a building. Angie felt a pang of insecurity. I'm just not lovable enough for a man like Matt.* Angie lamented aloud. There are warts I see every day in myself. I'm not too fond of these warts. If he saw them, he wouldn't like me either."

She talked briefly to her mother and father later in the morning, but they seemed so hurried that the conversation was disappointing. She had to accept they had a life, too. Loves and kisses over the phone were all they had time to share before they were off.

When evening came, Angie finished her last work on the table and packed it away. Though she would toss and turn all night, Thursday would arrive. A wish for a prince would rise again in Angie's dreams. Would her fairytale prince finally come by land or by sea? She eventually fell asleep, allowing her dreams to carry her through until sunrise.

The doorbell rang just as Angie had taken her fingers through her hair after the last roller. She gave herself one last glance over in the mirror and went for the door. Angie peeked through the peek hole and saw a pink-colored petal stopping her gaze further. When she opened the door, Matt greeted her with a bouquet he bought at the market on the way into town.

"This is for starters to get me in the door," Matt teased. "I am so glad I know the right people. Parking anywhere on the peninsula today is cruel. There are lots of people every. That's why I have plans to take you away and still enjoy the city."

"That sounds like a winning idea. You said to bring shorts, beach stuff, a dress up, and comfortable wear for hanging inside and outside. I did my best." Angie smiled and picked up a stuffed, colorful duffle bag.

"Looks good! And Belle, have we found a place for the floppy-eared 'muncher'?"

Angie giggled. "Yes, she is spending the weekend with my friend Stella and her family. She has kids who will love to care for Miss Belle and all her antics."

"It's warm, but would you like to walk up to the battery with me? Maybe you'd like to take a few photographs?"

"Okay, I'm game. I want to take you past a few streets and show you something. It keeps saying something to me. I don't know what it's saying."

"So, are you hearing about ghosts from Charleston's past? Do you hear a whisper from the upstairs window or an icy touch that reaches for your hand as you jog by?" Matt teased.

"Stop. If you're going to tease me, I won't show."

"No, I want to see what has caught your eye?" Matt responded.

Angie picked up her keys and led them out of the door onto the street. Sounds and noises were everywhere. They passed by planters of flowers and watched for uneven sidewalks where the tree roots had raised the concrete slabs. Tourists and locals mixed on crowded streets. When Angie reached the street she was looking for, she pulled Matt closer to tell him what she saw without yelling over the sound of the passing horse and carriage. I showed you the white houses that belonged to the sisters here, but I wanted you to see something else I've noticed. On the back side of Angie's favorite house, there is a plaque saying that the home was once lived in by General Edward Hawke, who was part of the royal naval fleet. "He was my 11th-generation grandfather. Well, maybe he was a step grandfather, depending on whether I came from the first or second marriage. Then again, if he had already died, was he anything to me at all?"

"How nice to track down the home of one of your ancestors," Matt responded with a gentle smile. "Yes, I am aware of the plaque and some of the history of Captain Hawke." He did not elaborate, but Matt's eyes took on a mysterious sparkle. "Seems to be a lovely house. I'm sure your grandmother was a beautiful woman like you to have a man as grand as Captain Hawke to woo her."

"I think you're teasing me again, but I'm unsure how, so I'll not be insulted. It's so funny; I only knew of our family around the New York and Philadelphia areas, except those who became snowbirds. To think they once lived here is quite interesting." "Yes, very interesting that you should find your way back to those old haunts. But, no, my lovely lady, I would not insult you. Perhaps it's the company that you keep that needs to behave."

"There you go again. You are making cryptic remarks, I think. Do you know something I don't know?"

"Perhaps I know a lot of things that you might have no interest in, but the one thing I think you will be interested in is at the end of the street. Shall we?"

Angie looked at him quizzically but followed his lead. Sure enough, a colorful vessel was passing through the harbor on the way to the marina. It could easily be seen along the railings on the other side of the park. The schooner had sales depicting the logo of the research foundation that sponsored it. Although it was considered a larger vessel than the sloop, it was exquisite, especially when all the sails were out, and the crew wore their uniforms.

"This was a sweet vessel for the pirate because it was faster than the much larger merchant ships of the day. It's like driving in a professional car race. Someone can drive a five-speed on the floor that can cut through corners easily. Another competitor can drive a large station wagon. The station wagon can carry more cargo, but it's slower. That fast number can chase the station wagon down every time. The wagons' only defenders are big cannons or another ship that can bump the fast one off the track." Matt said with teasing in his voice.

That's the beauty of living by the sea. Sometimes we have these opportunities to see replicas of the tall ships that once attempted to master the oceans. Only fools would believe that. Amazingly, man has traveled by water since ancient times. If we could see what the ships experienced throughout the millennium, would we understand history like we do today, or would we change chapters that were not true?

Matt looked around the harbor. Another boat caught his eye. This one was not as decked out in colors and modern, but had just as much meaning for Matt. His appearance must have caught the eye of the pilot as he immediately took to the phone when he spotted Matt on the sidewalk that surrounded the battery. Matt saw another man on a balcony of a multi-storied building just to his right. This man had binoculars and was looking straight at Matt. *"What was this all about?"*

Angie took Matt's elbow and leaned in for a selfie with the two of them together and the waterway in the background. She brought Matt's attention back to her.

"I admire your skills of being so well read on many subjects. Unfortunately, I can't remember details from the morning meeting; you seem to carry so much in your mind each day. Does it ever need a day of rest?"

"Absolutely! The only thing I want to think about for the next few days is sharing my time with you. He lightly grazed her nose with a soft touch of his finger. You don't have to say or do anything to please me. Just being with you makes me extremely happy."

"That is so sweet! I'm sure you may change your mind by midnight, but I'm willing to be that girl for the next few hours, at least."

"You're teasing me now," Matt said and smiled. "It's time for us to head to the island, anyway. By the time we get back and pass through the traffic going on to the bridge and then out of the city limits, we'll be right on track to checking in and finding the beach. Before we do, I want to take a picture of you so I can remember you by the water, with your hair blowing in the wind and the sunlight highlighting those strands of gold. He tapped his fingers along the edge of her hairline. On the way back, we can pass the front of the two houses you like and take a shot there too. An apparition of an old soul might show up in the image?" Matt teased.

"Okay, that sounds good. Perhaps the image will be handsome like you!" Angie giggled.

"I bet the captain was!" Matt turned his head away to see if anyone was following. Unfortunately, the flow of pedestrians behind him made it difficult to figure out who was following him.

"He was a general," Angie corrected.

"Oh, I forgot." Matt smiled. "That must have been one of those slips of the tongue. It's time for us to head to the island, anyway. By the time we get back and pass through the traffic going on to the bridge and then out of the city limits, we'll be right on track for checking in and finding the beach."

"Okay, I'm ready."

Another couple was lovely enough to snap a picture of where Matt had teased Angie. Unfortunately, he wouldn't let her look at the picture. "Oh no, this one is just for me, so I can remember your face when I am lost at sea and need a siren to call me back to the one I love."

"I will not stop singing until you are in from the cold and safely home. My lantern waits and watches as I pray on the stars guiding your journey," Angie responded, as if speaking a rote verse from her Vesper book in college.

"Who sounds like a philosopher now?" said Matt.

"Smarty, I've read a few books on the train in my lifetime," Angie responded teasingly.

"I thought you were one of those lightweight girls who only knew about clothes and makeup. You have a mysterious side of you. I'm finding all kinds of fun stuff about you already! Our time together is going to make an eventful weekend." Matt responded and put his hand in hers for the rest of the walk back to the apartment.

When the couple returned to it, it was just before 3:00 PM. So, it was the perfect time to head on out to the island.

Matt loaded Angie's duffle bag in the back of his SUV, pushing over some personal items. The next thing they knew, they were on their way. The island was an hour away along a picturesque road. Deep water lots dotted the flat two-lane highway, canopied by moss hanging low from the oak trees. Stately, homes were nestled far back from the road, sitting close to the coves and waterways that lead to the open waters of the Atlantic. The paved road traveled through Matt's definition of the low country with its finest on display. The white and gray heron doted on the collections of water left by the low tide. Spots of amber marshes could be seen between the holes made between lined oaks that marked the passage through the marshes and fields that led to the next barrier island.

Tonight, that was where Matt planned to be with the person he felt so close to in just a few months. God had to have had some part of the coincidence. There was no other way to explain what had happened in so short of time with two strangers walking on this blue sphere called Earth.

Chapter 11

THIS ISLAND WAS a world away from the city noise of horns and ambulance sirens. Instead, on the private beach, one hears the songs of the seagulls and the beat of the tidewaters coming ashore and flowing back out to the expansive pool of water known as the Atlantic Ocean. Maps can't fully describe the diversity of the ocean's edge as it reaches a new continent, Angie thought. She recalled the sharp rocks off the coast of Maine and how a ship could run aground in the fog. Here, the cost was gentler, like landing against a pillow, compared to the rough edges of New England.

Matt added his knowledge of the surrounding terrain as they set up the umbrella and chairs on the sand. "The captains and pirates who knew the area well had firsthand experiences of the perils of the warmer waters of the southern shores." Matt had made it his expertise to understand the nautical history of the shores along the eastern shoreline. He also researched the ecological systems around each geographical area. He knew the quiet coves and brackish waters further inland from the salty waters of the area had their predatory dangers. The cold-blooded amphibians lay on the grassy mounds of lagoons and rivers, waiting to consume its next morsel that dared to disturb its sleep. Respect the innate traits created in these creatures as part of the ecosystem or risk fatal consequences.

"This is gorgeous," Angie said as she removed her coverup before heading to the beach.

"Yep, I could say the same thing," Matt responded, not talking entirely about the same topic.

She picked up a seashell from the sand that the high tide had just dropped. She put it back down and let the incoming tide and foam wash it. Then, a few feet more, a sand dollar was seen. It was like finding gems.

Matt caught up to her and pulled her further into the water. The salty sea swirled around their ankles as they walked along the shore. "It keeps our bodies from feeling so warm from the sun," said Matt.

"I like it." Angie smiled back. "I'm not one to be a beach goddess, laying by the pool all day, but brief moments of bliss like this are perfectly acceptable. It's like eating chocolate. If God didn't want us to eat it occasionally, why did he make the cocoa bean?"

"I will not agree or disagree. However, I will say that the sun goddess thing suits you well," Matt replied with a smile.

After a mile up along the beach, the couple strolled back to their beginning spot. After returning to the umbrella's shade, Matt pulled out a water flask and gave Angie the metal flask to drink from.

She took a sip and realized it was just cool water. So, she took a second sip and poured a light stream around her neck. She gave the flask back.

Matt took another swig. "Don't think I will take this baby on one of my dangerous dives. No way. Back to the plane model with no memories attached." He gave Angie a wink and smiled. Both sat down on their chairs with their legs stretched out to relax. A few minutes later, Matt thought he saw something on the horizon. "I think the boat is coming!" He grabbed the container in the beach bag and pulled out a pair of binoculars. He looked, adjusting the magnification. "There she is!" He gave the binoculars and pointed to where the masted ship was coming into view.

"Wow! The ships look so majestic out there in the sea. It's almost like seeing a ghost from the past reappear."

"Yes, it gives you that feeling. It's not a super large boat like those old cargo ships. Angie was made to be a faster ship. The sloops were even smaller, but the smaller boats were harder to catch because of their smaller size. They could hide in the coves and maneuver the rivers more easily. Those big cargo ships carried more guns and massive cargo loads on board. They couldn't do much else once they got to their destinations. They were too cumbersome to deliver goods inland and had difficulty outrunning the pirates and smaller craft that got their cargo to the eastern ports and waterways easier and faster. From my understanding, your family built both later in the 1800s, but early on, they typically built sloops and schoolers."

"How did you know that?" Angie looked over in amazement.

"I did my research on historical nautical information. It was in the documents I found."

"That's cool information. Do you think my family would have built something like that schooner?"

"Yeah, I think so. If it had exceptional cabinetry work, I could probably tell you about the apprentice who built it?"

"Really! That is impressive."

"Yes, he was. He helped build a home on a river in Virginia. He was called to the site specifically because of his skills. You can see his boat-building skills by how he timber-framed the house. That house still stands three hundred years later, so he must have known what he was doing."

Angie looked out at sea again. "You are so interesting. I feel like I've known you forever, and you're filling me with these stories I have treasured in my heart my whole life." She looked back at Matt with a serious face. "It's like I've been waiting for you all my life."

"I'm not sure about all that. I'm not as old as the pyramids, and I think there's a good chance that the Vikings had found a new world by the time I was born. If you were waiting for your soul mate since the fourth grade. I didn't start wanting to be around girls until high school—too much fun with sports. However, high school came and gone, and I got corrupted in college. Your dad wouldn't have allowed me to date you back then." Matt said teasingly. "Interesting about the timber framing, though."

"Yeah!"

"I keep forgetting your family was part of the Dutch shipbuilders' side. My folks were a mix of Scots and Irish kicked back to Liverpool for disturbances they made and sailed out of Londonderry. The sole gene pool was tossed on the shoulders of an indentured teenager working as a captain's boy. There he met the loveliest maiden for the very first time."

Angie put the binoculars down for a moment in her lap with astonishment. "How do you know all this? Are you making up this story?"

Matt responded, "No, I don't think so. I may have thought it was once, but now it was all true. Some stories are oral traditions, and some came from diaries and artifacts left. I am distracting you. Watch the ship as it passes us by. That will be the best view. I don't want you to miss it!"

Matt got up from the lounge chair and watched as it approached. It was a fine-looking schooner and will most likely get much attention as it sails to its new home in Wilmington. But unfortunately, Charleston is just a pit stop at its ultimate home where it belongs. Nestor and his crew did a fine job of replicating the schooner. Matt imagined its new captain was proud to take its wheel and steer it through the channel where it was built and out to the open sea.

Matt and Angie watched the schooner leave their field of view as it rounded the island's northern end. It moved closer to where it would moor for the night before entering the port tomorrow.

Matt gave Angie some privacy to change and prepare for the evening at his rented villa. He would find his way around the nearby hotel, take some quiet time to catch up on emails and texts, and be back in an hour and a half to change himself. Grooming on his part was not much needed, a shower, a clean white shirt, a bow tie just for the occasion, and a pair of pressed slacks. A navy-blue dinner jacket for formality was required for dinner at the restraint, and he was set at his finest.

When he returned to the villa, Angie, the second bedroom door, closed. He could hear the music playing in the background. He started his ritual and lingered for some pleasant fragrance in the bathroom when he entered for his cleanup tasks. If a bathroom can smell this good after she takes a bath, think of what her hair will smell like in the moonlight, he thought. He stored the fragrance in his mind as he showered and shaved.

By 6:30 PM, Matt and Angie were escorted to their table on the restaurant's patio. The candle was lit after being seated. Matt was quick to order the wine and the evening's entrée. From then on, they felt privacy, just the two of them watching the sunset move into darkness as they talked and enjoyed their meal.

Angie had decided that the red dress was the right choice. She did not want to wear black for a moment; that was made of a little girl's dreams. The bomb had its place, as Lauren educated Angie, but you must save it for the right moment.

Matt reached for a box from his pocket once the plates were cleared. "I thought you might like this," Matt said, as he moved his chair around to block the view from the rest of the terrace and only on him.

Angie could still gaze over to the dunes out of the ocean beyond. The stars were making their nightly show in the sky.

"I picked the one in the window at the jewelry store you said you liked when we walked that day in Charleston."

Angie teared up. "We hardly knew each other when you came that weekend."

"Yeah, I know. I thought it might be a mistake then, but something else told me it was the one I wanted. Later, I returned and had the jeweler hold it until I knew you better and could get your s*ize*. I measured from that little birthstone ring you always wear. Later, I emailed the store, and they customized the ring for you. *I had them engrave the inside message*, too."

Angie read the lyrics. "It was from an old song of the seventies that she liked. One day, she found an LP in her father's collection of things next to his diploma and a lettered football jacket in the garage. Angie later found a CD version at a classic record store selling music from all genres in Boston. He still plays the music occasionally when he's up in his office. He always laughed and said it was mood music. It's what fueled his creativity. I was a product of the created ambiance, he told her once, trying to embarrass her mother when her parents described their relationship when they were young."

"Of course, I told them it was too much information and forbade them to tell me more about the birds and the bees. I would learn it all from my older sister, who was happily married to a corporate accountant." Angie said with tears still in her eyes.

"Let's hope we have a more exciting story than a corporate accountant. I met quite a few, and they all seem so boring." Matt added with a tease.

"Just wait! I'm supposed to say yes now to something?"

"That was part of the plan. So, I'm giving you this with the expressed proposal that you promise to let me take you home with me and never part until we hold hands together, watching the sea from the stars above."

"You are messing up my makeup." Tears lined the rims of her eyes. "Yes, Matt Fitz, and if you ever want to renegotiate this contract, you better hope we are already up there. Otherwise, one of us is going south, and it's not me!" Angie teased.

Matt held her hand. "Done deal! It's a win all the way around!" After putting the ring on Angie's finger and the moment he went to kiss her. He felt a vibration in his pocket and attempted to ignore the distraction. He finished the kiss, but his mind was now distracted again. The sensation started back up again. Matt pulled out the offending object to place it face down on the table. However, one glance at the glass and Matt's focus quickly shifted to the red alert on the screen. Matt swiftly waved to the server and asked if the restaurant had a television. He was directed to one in the hotel's pub, across from the hotel's atrium.

Angie was startled by the abruptness of Matt's mood and actions. However, when she saw how serious he was, she followed his directions to wait while he swiftly escaped through the exit.

Inside the lounge area, there was more background noise. However, a big screen TV near the bar showed a news bulletin. A cruise ship and a smaller boat collided just beyond Charleston Harbor. The news channel reported approximately one thousand crew and passengers were on board the cruise liner. Evacuations were underway. More details were to follow.

Matt understood what the alert was for now. He made a quick call and rushed back to where he had had a magical moment just minutes before. "Angie, I must leave. I just received an alert. Please stay in the villa for me until I get back. I will give my keys to you. Someone is coming to take me to the command center. I have what I need in the back of my SUV. Please, stay. I will be back in a few hours, I'm sure. I will call you when I can, okay?" Angie looked at Matt with questioning eyes but saw the earnestness in his plea. "I do whatever you tell me." Good, he paid the server, who was coming swiftly, sensing urgency.

Fifteen minutes later, Matt was at one of the emergency command centers. From that location, Matt could be used on one of the rescue boats or aircraft vehicles based out of this center. He could also be taken to another destination where his skills were needed.

"Please don't worry, Angie. I'll be back as soon as possible. It will probably be only a few hours. Take this, and he handed her an envelope. Remember, you have my keys if something should happen. There are phone numbers inside if you need them." He kissed her again and quickly moved toward the building.

Angie watched as he ran inside with his gear. She was stunned at what was happening. Angie returned to the villa as directed. She turned on the TV. Similar reports were being reported on all the local network stations. Angie called her parents but only reached voice mail. Finally, she changed into shorts and a T-shirt and sat beside the television with her phone.

Matt texted a quick message to Angie a short time later. It read. *I am at the coastguard* station and deploying with a rescue team. Do not worry. I am a highly trained professional diver who frequently works with the military and local authorities.

Angie sat watching the news, but little new information was being released on the network and cable stations. She walked out to the beach with binoculars to see what she could see. She noticed a great deal of light and smoke in the sky north of where she was. Helicopters hovered in the air around the same area. A few others had joined her on the beach, and they shared updates as more people came. Occasionally, a watercraft would pass in the ocean beyond the resort—some larger than others, but all were going in a similar direction. As time passed, medical helicopters traveled overland in the opposite direction. Angie wondered if they had injured passengers or where they were going home because they were not needed. She said and prayer for Matt and those affected by the collision. Would they need more help, and what kind of help was needed? She prayed for Matt's safety. Angie didn't receive an instant answer to prayer, but she saw a star shine brightly above her in the sky. Had heaven heard their requests in the middle of a dark beach with the ocean's roar drowning their voices? Angie thought deeper. God has always been present. The sea and stars have always been there, even *when she wasn't listening. Please protect him and give him a sign that lets me know I love him.*

Chapter 12

MATT ASSESSED THE situation from up above as the helicopter approached the scene. The collision occurred within the twelve-mile United States coastal jurisdiction. The bow of the private yacht had swiped the larger ship. Although the larger ship was afloat, it was difficult to tell the damage to the hull. The vessel had one hundred people as guests. That would mean they abandoned the yacht, which took more damage and appeared to be sinking in the bow. Matt estimated that at least twelve rubber rafts for guests should have been accessible. There were not that many rafts on the water. Some had capsized during the evacuation. Others floated beyond what the eye could see, or never deployed. If any had gotten a clean break early, other rescue parties would have reached them by now. The captain remained prudent with the craft for as long as possible, and no one was scrambling in a panic. Other crew members were climbing on a raft with speed but not chaotic, pushing and shoving. The captain hung back, reluctant to leave the ship from what Matt could see. That might be an honorable gesture, but not prudent if all had been accounted for and were off the ship. *Why was he hesitating to leave with the last raft of the crew? Was he waiting for someone?* Matt watched again from the open door. The captain returned to the cabin and brought something out a few minutes later. It looked like a metal case, somewhat larger than a laptop case or briefcase. He looked about him again as if he was waiting for someone *or thing to pick him up. He had been avoiding the rafts with others by batting those options away with a nudge.* Matt assumed he would not be afraid of a safety raft if he was a boat captain. Matt continued to study the scene more. A swimmer from the copter was lowered to reach a fallen victim from one of the life rafts. It appeared the women panicked when the raft moved with the wave. With a harness, the swimmer could reach the victim, be harnessed with the swimmer, and be guided to the larger boat just yards away as she floated with the life jacket in place.

Matt watched the movement of the captain again. He had inflated a raft and tied it to a pulley to lower it to the water's surface. The pilot wasn't rowing to the coastguard's boat. And he wasn't paddling towards the harbor where masses of support were assembling. He is behaving strangely. Indeed, Matt thought and relayed the information to the coastguard on deck. Watch for a boat or device on the water that could intercept him. I bet my fly-fishing gear that the suitcase does not contain a second pair of dry underwear. Can you give this message to the pilot?

Matt kept his telescopic lens on the raft. You've done it this time, Hugh. That's why you and your crew have followed me. I didn't want to know about your side job. Matt could see a small boat moving toward the open water. It did not appear to be in search of victims. As the boat got closer, Matt was fairly sure he knew the vessel. However, it was moving away from the man in the raft, and it was moving away from the hovering helicopter. Instead, it was making a run for the open water of the sea. Matt looked down at the man in the raft and saw his expression. He believes there was a security net left for him, but it vanished. Hugh alone to face himself in those lonely moments floating a drift, abandoned by his crew and those he trusted. His strength could not take him back where others could pull him. There was only up. Matt caught the face of the broken man. Matt put the camera down and closed his eyes for just a few seconds. Ask the pilot permission to lower me down to bring the man up. "

"Sir, given his behaviors, we don't know if he is dangerous!"

"I know, but I don't believe his is. The man is someone I know. He will listen to me," Matt said soberly.

"That's crazy!" said the other rescuer.

"Yes, it's that too. While I get ready. There's a phone in that bag. Never mind. They'll know."

Matt monitored the scene below as he harnessed up and put his gear on.

After a few minutes, the helicopter was moving into position. It blasted a voice down to the man below with a large beam of light shining.

"Swimmer going down."

Slowly, Matt dropped from the chopper, intent on completing his mission. As he reached the raft, he called for the hand of the man. "Take this, Hugh, and put it around you. You will need to hold on to me as you lift yourself into the coming basket. Once you get in, it will lift you."

"Why are you doing this? Why did you come to save me when there were all the others?" Bitters asked despondently.

"I wasn't coming for you. Maybe something caused us to find you. I don't know. We are here to take you to safety. Think about that right now," Matt responded.

"They'll condemn me for this, but I swear I didn't wreck the yacht into the passenger ship. I'd never do that. I've done my share of *bad things*. But I wouldn't have harmed anyone."

"Wait till will get you out of this boat and safe. Then you can share what happened." A few seconds later, the basket hit the water. Hugh positioned himself to reach for the metal cage-like structure with a seat. The metal suite case taken from the damaged yacht slid off the raft into the ink-black sea. Matt hadn't missed the intentional maneuver. But that wasn't his priority now. Hugh then climbed into the metal rescue basket and sat down. Matt gave the signal, and the basket lifted towards the helicopter. Matt's turn followed as he held on to the cable. It would feel good to get warm again. Holding the young woman sitting in front of a fire pit underneath a blanket of stars he hastily left just a few hours ago would feel even better. "How did you get the mark on your eye?" Matt asked. He saw the reddened area around the orbital bone.

"Someone hit me and knocked me out. Something happened on board. There were some sounds behind me, and I went to turn around to look. Then a couple of men came to the pilot's area. I do not remember anything else until I woke up and people climbed into rafts. The giant wall of the passenger liner was all I saw when I came to, and I figured we must have hit it. I wasn't at the controls when it happened. Someone knocked me out before we got that close."

Matt saw the hesitation and the chaos that must be in the boat captain's mind.

Hugh's eyes started to tear up. He covered his face with his gnarled and calloused hands, hiding the emotions of a man who experienced many disappointments. This evening was another failure in his life. He felt the emotional chain of bitterness tightening in his gut. "Why did you come for me?" Hugh's voice was low and gruff.

"We didn't come for you. Our job was to rescue anyone who needed help and was in danger."

"I didn't need help. You should have left me to die out there."

Matt responded in a low, quiet voice. "They left you, Hugh. Whoever you believed would give you protection abandoned you.

I'm not a priest or a judge, Bitters, so you don't have to say anything to me." Matt hoped he wouldn't talk until they reached the checkpoint.

"My crew left me. I'm not worth more than shark bate to those guys. They are a bunch of rats, all of them," Bitters lamented.

Matt tried to hold back the cliché words that rolled out of his mouth. "You are getting a second chance, Hugh. Take it!"

"You're thinking bad of me, I know, not that it matters. But it never seems like I can get ahead. No matter how hard I work to turn my life around, I get kicked in the head. Somebody's always there to fill me up."

Matt tried to listen to the man's rambling with compassion. "I've not been in your shoes, Bitters, so I won't judge. But I am frustrated with trying to make things happen. I sometimes look at the tools I'm using to get what I want. I have felt disappointment, Bitters. If we let it, it will eat you and me on the inside like acid. I need to look for help to find the right tool meant for me and accept that as a gift."

"You think you are so smart when you've been given everything in life?" Bitters grumbled some more.

Matt stayed silent to allow the older man to ramble. But in his mind, Matt's thoughts were present, leading him to respond to the situation. "I learned to be humble enough to know I don't need everything. I can't get it from my work, and I can't get it from a beautiful woman. Money is a powerful tool, but I'm a fool with it if

I'm not seeking the right way to use it. I've been a fool many times and am not proud of it. There's also the reality of what I do with my life when I am desperate, and there only look like bad choices. One of those choices will make someone else unhappy, and the snowball begins." Matt stopped for a moment. *Did Bitters need to hear these words or were they for himself?* "I can't tell anyone what to do in those moments. But I know those moments are when my life changes. There's an ingredient that I don't have on my own. I don't think you do either, Bitters. I don't think any of us do. Guys on that yacht may have looked like they had it all together with their polished looks and filled wallets. But my hunch is that they didn't have either. They left you cold and at risk of drowning in the night."

Bitters rubbed his eyes some. Then, after several minutes of silence, he began. "You know, I was trying to protect you. You've always done right by me. So, I wanted to return the favor," Bitters replied.

"When? I don't know what you're talking about. You shouldn't say anything more until the medical staff sees you."

"It was me who kept my guys following you in Charleston."

"Oh boy, you're not going to be quiet, are you?" Matt said. "I am closing my eyes until we reach our destination." Mat laid his head on the backrest of his seat and feigned sleep.

"I didn't want you to know about the shipwreck," Bitters remarked.

Matt opened his eyes with full attention. "What shipwreck?"

"The one off the coast near the plane crash," Bitters responded. "The one you were going back out to check on near the unnamed island."

"What do you know about a shipwreck near the crash site?" Matt asked with interest.

"I know it's there. That's all I'm going to say." The older man shivered under the blanket.

"Was it British or American?" Matt asked.

"I don't know for sure. I'd say, by the size of the remains, it was a frigate. Most likely British, not much of the hull or masts remains. Looks like it went down blazing. It doesn't look like a storm knocked it down. I would say that treasure hunters have gotten to anything worth anything by now. It's not marked as a protected area yet. I suspect you were suspicious that you found something. Rumor had it you had reported a probable location of a wreck to the authorities when you were working on that plane crash off the island above St. Mary's. You are about following the laws, and I have my ears out for the buzz around the coast from Virginia down the coast. I suspect you have more interest in the site than most. I didn't want you snooping around when the bad guys were out. They do some trafficking out past the 12-mile border, but they come closer to shore when they smell fresh fish on the market, if you know what I mean. So, I tagged you to ensure you didn't go anywhere close when I knew they might be nearby." Matt closed his eyes again after Bitters had related his information. It was time to sink this all in and solve tonight's puzzle even more unexpectedly of how the information just received aligned with the truth three hundred years ago.

Once the chopper reached its designated spot-on land, everyone departed the aircraft. Medical personnel were waiting and took Hugh to a medical facility nearby. It would give the crew and aircraft time to refuel and prepare for the next mission. Matt picked up his gear and went inside the station. Matt was sure there would be more pages to the story of the events of the evening. For now, he was ready to rest at the command center. His first thoughts were to call Angie. Then his father and mother, who Matt knew would watch the news updates on television. What a rumple in his romantic plans for the weekend! He would make this up to Angie. Maybe he couldn't go back and give her the memory of their missed engagement celebration. But he would think of a way to celebrate their commitment.

It was still early morning when he texted his father and Angie again. She told him she was at her apartment and would explain later. He looked at his phone, showing Angie had been sending texts for most of the night.

One of the local divers he knew from the past and who collaborated with him to check out the structure of the yacht and ship gave him a ride *back to Angie's place. Matt saw his* SUV parked in the small driveway beside Angie's apartment. He found a spare key she had left him outside, and he snuck inside in the early hours just as dawn reached the horizon over Charleston harbor. The lights were on, and chattering came from the living room. Matt could smell fresh coffee. He dropped the keys on the table, and before he could walk to the end of the hallway, Angie came bolting out of the kitchen to run toward him. They embraced for what seemed like several minutes.

"I hear voices," Matt whispered in her ear.

"It's my parents," Angie replied. "They were on the cruise liner that collided with the yacht last night. They're fine. It's a long story, but they said that the crew on the ship were wonderful with preparing the passengers and not panicking after the collision. After a couple of hours, the tugboats pushed the yacht away from the liner, and they cleared the ship to come into port. They said there was no chaos on board."

"Are they okay?" Matt asked.

"Yes, the passengers on the yacht probably felt more of the jar of the collision. My parents saw a lifeboat speeding away just before the yacht hit the cruise liner. I'm not sure what that was about. My parents said it was too dark to see how many were inside the boats. The lifeboat sailed to another close boat to be rescued from the salty waters. They left a few others on the yacht after it crashed into the liner. Some went into another group of lifeboats and appeared to be picked up by a coast guard craft. My parents did not see anyone that looked hurt."

"All very interesting," Matt responded. He held Angie's hands and stroked over the ring finger with the diamond he had given her last evening. "I'm still cold from diving. Let me get some coffee and take another hot shower. I'll be more sociable after my liver isn't shivering against my lungs and my stubble is gone," he joked. They both walked toward the smell of a fresh pot of brewed coffee.

"My parents took a shuttle provided by the cruise line to a church used as a staging center last night because many things were not open when they arrived. All the hotels were booked because of the festival. I told them I would take them to the airport to pick up a rental car after they rested. We were waiting here awhile, hoping to get a message from you. I waited long on the resort beach, watching lights, planes, and helicopters in the sky. Finally, I met when I got the text from Dad. I loaded yours and my things into your SUV and drove to pick them up. It was best to bring them here, at least for tonight, and ensure they didn't need anything. I didn't return the villa keys, though. I wasn't sure what was happening."

Matt replied, "I am so sorry to mess up our time together this weekend. It's fortunate that there were only a few minor injuries from what I know, and you reached your parents. I took a second mission on the cruise liner and dived with several other divers. The cruise boat didn't look to have any issues other than cosmetics. I hope it wasn't a terrible fright for everyone on board."

"Me too. Your things are in my room. Now that you are here, I can take them to get the car whenever they are ready. I don't want them to feel cooped in after their wild night. Thank you for asking them to come down. For the weekend. That was extremely sweet."

Before entering the little kitchenette, Matt kissed her on the forehead. "You are an angel. Let me say hello to your parents, and I will take you up on crashing for a while as long as you or your parents don't need me for anything."

She touched his wavey hair. "No, all is fantastic now that you're back."

Several hours later, Matt and Angie were back off the island where they had started on Thursday evening, feeling refreshed and mischievous. Matt asked, "Do you think your parents will think we are rude that we snuck away to be alone today?" He followed Angie's lead as he tipped his oar into the water.

Angie kept her balance and rhythm steady as she pushed and guided the paddleboard she was standing on in a smooth glide across the water. "Not at all. They were young once, too, and were quite a romantic couple. Even now, they still hold hands when they go to dinner. It's hard to think of one's parents that way, but that's who they are. I've always felt comfortable with the little things they do to keep their romance going. I suspect my mom has a baby doll lingerie in her suitcase."

Matt laughed. "If my mother went packing for a weekend with my dad, it would not be a baby doll nightgown. It would look more like a flannel from neck to toe. If there were a pair of matching thermal pajamas, she'd have them underneath. She's never warm, even in the heat of summer. Menopausal hot flashes would be a blessing from God for her."

"You are being bad, as I know your parents are lovely people," Angie responded.

"I didn't say she was ugly! She's just cold all the time." Matt smiled.

"You are a complete mess; a wonderful, fun, and intelligent mess. However, you are a nonsensical mixture of DNA, and I love it!" Angie teased.

"I hope your mother passes on the trait about the pretty pajamas packed away in vacation luggage. Shoot, you can pack them in a little bag after the dishes. I could appreciate it on some nights. I see some advantages of marrying a Van Dorn daughter now. Speaking of clothing, have I seen the 'bomb' that Ms. Lauren helped you find?"

Angie's mouth flew open. "How did you know about that?" Angie kept her eyes forward but smiled.

"Let's just say I watched you walk into that store on the main street, and then I watched you come back out with a bag. That's the only thing that boutiques sell, so I suspect my chances are pretty good that I'll get to see it sometime. Also, your friend Lauren teased you about the 'bomb' on the phone before we left. Do you remember? I assumed you already had it in your bags."

Angie lowered the ore to slow her board and let Matt pull parallel. "The response to your assumption is yes," Angie teased.

"That's the answer I was hoping to hear!"

The couple continued to glide down the calm salty sound that created a watery buffer between the shores of the two islands. They returned to the villa to escape the sun several hours later. Matt reached the shaded patio, stretched out on a lounge chair, and began reading a book. Angie phoned her parents to check in on them.

"You know your father, Angie. He wanted to go over and see the ships in the harbor, so we walked along the pier and down along the marina. Somehow, we met someone in passing, and we got to talking. One thing led to another, and we started talking about you and you and Matt and how we had come down to celebrate your engagement. Well, the boat owner in the marina said he knew Matt and the owner of the three-masted schooner in the harbor. He even implied that he and his wife were planning to meet up with you and Matt for dinner, and then something came up, and the plans were changed. The owner of the schooner offered to show us the boat since we were friends of Nestor and Matt. Your father was in heaven. He looked at everything on the ship. I was afraid your dad would say we needed to buy one just like this, and I would have to give him a reality check. However, he was content with just looking at it for today. That made me happy. It made him agreeable whole the whole day. It was a very humid afternoon, so we went to the museum. We saw the civil war relic you talked about in the magazine article. Your father loved that, too, with all his work at the academy and his love for history. We've just been having fun. We toured one of the house museums near the balcony as it was close by. The piazzas are breathtaking as you stand and gaze out into the harbor. The walk through the historic district is just fantastic. Then, we saw the ship we left New York on. There was a lot of activity around the boat. Your father wanted to get as close as we could take photos, but they wouldn't let us come any closer than the parking lot. Sweety, did you have a fun and relaxing day?"

"Yes, Mother. Matt and I are having a wonderful time. He is rested and is ready to go anywhere. We want you and Dad to come over for supper."

"That's lovely, dear, but you and Matt have barely had time alone."
"Mother, we want to share time with you and Dad!"

"We will spend the whole day with you tomorrow based on what Matt's father mentioned when he called, so maybe that will be too much."

"Are you kidding me? By now, you've grown on me, and I'm sure Matt also wants to talk with Dad some more."

Matt chimed in. "I have a better idea. I must change our cars, so let's meet there, and we'll walk up the street and grab something casual. Then, if it's too busy, we will order and pick it up."

"That's fine. We don't want to be any burden. We are happy to entertain ourselves. Your father and I plan to drive down to Matt's place at about 10:00, and we will be happy to help Matt's parents get everything set up. The little engagement party will be so much fun. We'll meet some of your friends we could reach on such short notice." "How do you know all our friends?" Angie asked.

"We have connections, darling," her mother replied.

Angie could hear the giggle in her mother's voice. "Why do I feel something is up? But I am game!" Angie said.

"Don't think of doing anything for tomorrow! We are going to keep things family-style and straightforward, just like we do when the Van Dorn clan gets together back home. We'll have some great food, some things people can do, and enjoy the company. Your new in-laws seem like such friendly people, and we have many things in common."

"Okay, Mother. They set the plan. Matt and I will be over around 6:00 PM. We can all walk to the restaurant. I will make the reservations. We'll do something casual. If that fails, we'll order some carryout. That's the plan."

"Okay, dear. We'll see you tonight. Bye."

That evening, Matt sat across from Angie's dad at the restaurant. The food and acoustics were good, allowing everyone to converse around the table. The place had a cozy feeling. A few patrons had on uniforms. Several cadets from the military school close by were with family and friends. A birthday celebration was happening a few tables away.

Angie sat and enjoyed the ambiance. The restaurant was like a place her parents would have chosen back home. Matt and Angie's father told the group their stories of their days and nights at the academy. Mrs. Van Dorn was also witty and engaged in many of the topics that went around the table. Matt's dad would have enjoyed being part of the stories. Angie was getting suspicious that this trio at the table were not strangers, though nothing was left out of the bag yet. The more she smiled and enjoyed her wine, the more the warm fuzzy feelings turned towards the suspicion. *It was no accident that her father had her ask for an interview with Mr. Matt Fitz for the article. These three adults around the table were in cahoots. How lovely to know that her most beloved, trusted people were diabolical in scheming for a plan she knew nothing about. Something smelled very fishy about this table, and it was the shrimp cocktail.* Angie's smile remained glued to her face. But her mind raced to figure out the connection between their intentions.

"Matt, I would like to see some of those old nautical pieces left to you. It's interesting to have so many family pieces in one collection. Maybe tomorrow, while we are at your place, I can still meet you for a few minutes, and you can show me what you have. Also, maybe we can exchange notes on my research."

"Absolutely," Matt said without elaborating.

Angie caught that quick silence. Matt had elaborated on everything he spoke about this evening. Although, on the one subject, she knew he could talk for hours about to someone, he remained quiet. She felt *confused. Everyone at this table is playing poker and knows each other's hand, even mine. Still, I don't know what anyone has, Angie thought—the evening ended a couple of hours after they returned to Angie's apartment.*

"I'm going to drive my car to the island tonight and take it to Matt's place tomorrow. That way, Matt can stay there, and I can return here. It will work better that way.

"Okay, I'll follow behind. We'll see you all in the morning?" Matt said as he opened the door to Angie's car and allowed her to enter. Then, Matt moved towards his vehicle and climbed in. "We'll see you at sunrise tomorrow."

"We'll see you both tomorrow!" Angie's parents said and waved goodbye. The Van Dorns walked back to the apartment with arms around each other's waists.

"We did good," said Mrs. Van Doren

"We only helped to move the dots closer a little. But it's more than us that makes the connection." Her husband said and winked.

Angie and Matt returned for their last night at the villa. Both were tired from the day's events, including the early morning drama.

Matt thought the night had gone terrific, thought this was the night of the bomb. He dropped his keys on the counter and walked to the screen to look at the stars and catch the dotted lights on the horizon. "Come and look, Angie. The lighthouse is about thirty miles from here and probably close to the halfway point from my house to here."

"Yes, I saw it last night on the beach, watching the emergency helicopters fly overhead. You know we haven't talked a lot about last night.

"I'm just trying to piece together who you are, Matt."

"I'm not that complicated, Angie. Come here."

Angie responded by moving into his arms.

"Angie, I don't have a shocking past. I told you what happened to my first fiancé. My father and your father met several years ago because they sought information about the same thing. It is about history, our families, and facts. I grew up and pieced pieces together on my own. My work sometimes gives me more clues, like last night. I have a new clue, and I need to assemble it with the other clues. That is what my father and your father have been doing for many years. They've spent so much time interacting that they became friends, and so have my mother and your mother." Matt said.

Angie looked at Matt and saw his sincerity. She knew he wanted to tell the story so it wouldn't be an issue of trust.

"I think your parents and my parents had always hoped we would meet each other one day and bring our families together. I was dating someone else at the academy, so your father did not encourage us to meet. Plus, you were younger. Instead, he befriended me since my return to civilian life. He would talk about his beautiful daughter and how accomplished she was. I didn't process everything, but I stored it somewhere. I didn't want to be in a relationship, but eventually I yearned for something I remembered and loved in Naya. Was it still alive in this world and could God still be alive?" Matt took Angie's hand and continued. "My father would share things too, but not about you specifically. He wanted me to find the one that was meant for me." Matt reached up to brush a tendril away from her eyes. "When the opportunity came, your father shared my contact information with you. I had never seen you in person. But when you walked into my office and looked around, I had a feeling you were someone different. You stood out from the crowd of people that I engage with each day. I saw the signs and hoped you were thinking the same thing."

"Wow, that's a lot to digest.," Angie replied.

Matt hesitantly answered the questions. "Yes, it is a lot. I don't know if your parents are close friends, but I had some conversations and correspondence with them. Your father was an instructor of mine, so we have had a professional relationship for a few years now. In addition, my parents and your parents have met in the past. There were reasons from a professional standpoint that they met up. Probably, they ran into each other accidentally, too."

"Are you going to reveal the elephant you're trying to hide because it is glaringly looking at me?" Angie said in frustration.

"Tomorrow, when we get together, you'll find out more. I'm not sure what I know. I'm still sorting out some things myself. But it's an old story that wants the truth to be told."

"I guess I have to wait till tomorrow to hear more, don't I?" Angie asked.

"I hope you will patiently wait and understand. It's not that it matters how I feel about you. That won't change. But you may want to know who I am and where I came from to decide on your own. It's your choice, Angie, and no one is taking that away from your parents, not my parents and not me. Once I met you, I knew it as if I had known you all my life."

"You're making me a little scared, Matt. But I will trust you until I learn more." Angie looked up at the sky and saw the star she had seen the night before.

Chapter 13

THE SMALL GET together at Matt's place turned into a back, front, and side yard full of people. Matt and Angie's dad put a volleyball net up in the yard. He purchased some extra-large beach balls at a store coming into town. Mr. Van Dorn figured it was safer to spike and pummel the teammates with these than the traditional ball; he wanted to keep the groom as safe as possible. Jarl and Lauren led Team Barracuda, while Stanley and Mary from the law firm formed Team Stingray. The team that reached fifty points was the winner. Achieving the points was a scandalous affair for both teams. First, a back pass to Angie's 6-foot three father standing on the sidelines hit the ball out of bounds on the opponent's side, which should have been a foul. Matt refused to listen to Team Barracudas' argument for fair play. Then there was a sneaky point earned after a sliding player hit the beach ball on a bounce, where it ricocheted off a cooler into Angie's hands. She bopped it to Ben, who walked it up to the net and spiked it to the other side. Voices were shouting foul.

Matt, who acted as the judge, ruled that all fair in beach ball. The group voices went up, claiming unfair advantage after the judge went and kissed Angie after he told her, "Nice one."

Team Stingrays had their cries of unfairness as well. Jarl connected the leaf blower to the extension cord and cleared his side of the court whenever a ball came close to the net. The teams finally settled in a truce with a tie at 11 points each.

For those who wanted less excitement in the sun, a game of bridge was happening on the screen porch. This group was a little less raucous, but now less animated in the stories being told around the table.

By late afternoon, all were sweaty, tired, and well-fed. The group melted away, and by 5:00 PM, everyone had left the premises of 84 Starboard Lane except for Matt's and Angie's parents. A group of helpers stayed around to fold the tables and chairs. Matt and his father brought the garbage bags to the curb to pick them up the next day. The dishwasher scoured the dishes while Angie and Matt's mother put things ready to go back in the cabinets and closets in stacks. It was a well-organized system, and Matt's and Angie's mother's plan for kitchen workflow was rolling smoothly. After everything was back in place, Matt loaded up his father's truck with the things returning to the storage unit. While there, Matt invited Mr. Van Dorn to see some of the family items he had. They shared stories about what they knew that tied each piece together with the other family's stories. When they returned, Angie was dying to know what she had missed. She knew the discussion between both families was part of the hidden agenda for tonight's sit-down meeting before everyone dispersed.

In the meantime, she was happy to bring Sam home from the neighbors. He pranced and rolled, feeling out his old digs. Finally, the dog pulled a sweatshirt from the laundry basket onto the laundry room floor. Sam carried the garment into the living room, where the furry creature curled over the top until Matt came home. But Angie had to admit Matt was having the same effect on her. She was missing her friend and companion as well.

A brief time later, the guys came home, and they could relax. Matt's parents were staying overnight. Angie's parents made plans to stay back on another famous island. Angie would be the only one driving back to Charleston alone to get back into her school and work routine. She didn't care when she got in, as her day tomorrow was light. "This is a delightful spot to plant me! I think it was so much fun today," Mrs. Fitz responded as she sat on one of the overstuffed short couches.

Matt said, "It was, and thanks go to all of you. Of course, Angie and I weren't expecting you to fuss over our engagement. But we appreciated it, and I think everybody had a great time!"

"Yes, you gave us a gift of happy memories!" Angie added.

"It's something we wanted to do. That includes all your friends that came."

Matt sat on the floor and pulled Angie down with him. He massaged her shoulders.

"That's good."

"Okay, so Angie's been a little irritable the last few days because she thinks we have left out. I want to be honest and tell her the truth, so she doesn't feel left out of the mystery. So, we'll start with question number one. Did my parents know each other before today? Who wants to answer?"

"I will take that." Mr. Fitz said. "The answer is yes. When Matt was at the academy, I met your father, Mr. Van Dorn, at one of the school's social events. Since then, we have run into each other, exchanged emails and correspondence, and, from time to time, had dinner with our wives present."

"Thank you, Dad, for your honesty."

"The second question is, have you attempted to provide photos or other information about each other's children to manipulate the outcome of Angie's and my relationship? Answer truthfully."

"I can say that absolutely no photos were given to Mr. Fitz or his son from us directly." Mr. Van Dorn looked at his wife to check if she agreed and did so. He had a smug on his face that Angie suspected was a truthful, albeit camouflaged, response.

"Angie, are there questions you want to ask those before you?" Matt asked.

"Yes, I do," she said with a sarcastic look. "Did any of you create a plan to get Matt and me together?"

"She goes for the bullseye on her first shot!" Matt said.

All looked at each other and raised their hands halfway. "Guilty," they all said simultaneously.

Mrs. Van Dorn was the first to please her case. "Dear, it wasn't a plan. It was more like an idea that happened, and one thing led to another. With you deciding to move to Charleston, we all had similar ideas. So, we each said it would be nice if you and Matt would get together. The article for the magazine was perfect. We didn't need to do anything. We just let nature take its course."

Mrs. Fitz added. "You are a beautiful, accomplished young lady, and Matt is a successful, handsome young man. We raised smart children. We had faith that you wouldn't pass up on something special." "Well said!" Mr. Van Dorn chimed in.

"Any further questions?" Matt asked as he looked at Angie with a smile.

"Yes, one more. What does our family history have to do with us?" Angie asked, waving her hand between Matt and herself.

"She missed her calling in life. As a prosecuting attorney, she would put fear down my spine," Matt teased. "Mr. Van Dorn, let's ask you for an answer."

"That question is still being investigated?"

Angie looked at her father, questioning. "Is Matt like my half-brother or something?"

"Of course not. What we know is a story, an oral tradition of sorts that blends Matt's family with our generations ago. We've been exploring what each side of the family has that would prove or disprove information regarding our ancestors several generations back.

"Is there something weird, like an ancestor was an alien, and he impregnated a maiden in the family tree?" Angie asked sarcastically.

"She's good; she's throwing aces today," Matt joked.

"Come on, guys, I am joking about aliens. That is true. There are no aliens, right?" Angie teased.

Mr. Fitz responded. "Absolutely, no outer space aliens. Our family roots are just as solid a part of this planet as the Van Dorns."

Matt chimed in. "Wow, I'm glad we proved that rumor wrong."

"Honey, we are talking about a family connection back three hundred years ago regarding Captain Hill. I believe Matt has a painting of him somewhere as part of the heirlooms from the family."

"True, a copy is in my office. That is what Angie has seen. Her father saw that today. However, the real painting is upstairs in the room I call the library," Matt responded.

"Some documents from an English Captain portray Captain as a pirate and scoundrel. However, that contradicts some documents, stories, and rumors that persist today. Some information would lead one to believe he was a quiet hero that helped the colonies win the battle with England. Perhaps the actual truth is somewhere in between." Mr. Fitz stated. "Your father and I have shared documents and information over the years. Your family and my ancestors may have been intertwined previously."

"How many generations are we talking about?" Angie asked.

"Nothing recent. We are talking about the twelfth or thirteenth generation back. Nothing to worry about," Mrs. Fitz added, looking at her hands.

Angie responded, "That's good."

Matt broke into the conversation. "I wanted you to see some things in the library while you were here. I'll bring them down." A few minutes later, Matt came downstairs with a box. "These are just some personal items like the compass, an eyepiece, and a journal on his journey as an indentured sailor aboard the merchant ship Gibraltar. It was a Norwegian-built vessel with an English Name, but we know it left Londonderry, Ireland, for America. So, it's interesting how that meshed."

Matt's father chimed in. "When I started digging into the family history. I discovered that Luke Shaw had been indentured and served as an apprentice to Silas Van Dorn, a shipbuilder out of the Philadelphia area. He came over on the same ship as the Van

Dorn sisters. Thomas James Hill learned to build sloops and schooners, bringing trade to America. He also worked in the Philadelphia area, making boats around the same time. Both builders started building sloops and schooners. They were better equipped to navigate trade in the rivers and along the coastline in the colonies. The big merchant ships couldn't reach the trading points inland, so there was a real market for these smaller vessels. Thomas knew this kind of boat and what it could do."

"The Van Dorns also knew this and built a family dynasty on shipbuilding. Eventually, they received military contracts to build ships for what we now know became the U.S. Navy. Then, of course, they ventured into other industries when things changed, but that's how they started based on what I could glean."

Angie's' father chimed in. "That's what I have found out myself. Thomas Hill is an interesting person in the family tree. Unfortunately, there are some holes in the story that I haven't been able to fill in."

Angie's father added what he knew. "The Van Dorn family boarded the ship in Londonderry. The Dutch and English were not on good terms then, so I'm not sure how the boat was in a British controlled area with a Norwegian beginning. Perhaps that is an interesting story to research, too. It's not quite clear why that was their point of departure. Perhaps the father had military connections. They also were a religious family, and some groups organized transportation for immigrants of different faiths. Given some personal accounts found, I suspect those on that trip had that background. There is an entry in the ship's log of the two Van Dorn sisters and three sons. They were young girls at the time of the ship's crossing. The youngest must have made an impression on the younger shipmate. His name was Luke Shaw. Personal correspondence that has been documented infers a friendly, if not affectionate, attachment early on. After that, however, their lives took on different paths."

Matt looked at Angie for a moment. "I bet she was a stunner like you."

Angie blushed and nudged her father on the knee to continue the conversation.

"Matt's family has more information about the captain. I do have notes that his trade was a shipbuilder first. He eventually became a captain of the Continental Navy. Perhaps the British Captain Hawke had a negative mark on young Luke's back. Their animosity seems overly fueled with hatred. The youngest Van Dorn sister married Captain Hawke. That gives an interesting piece to the story."

"I showed you the two sister's homes in Charleston near the Battery," Angie said. "They both took my attention soon after I moved to Charleston. Matt has seen them, too."

Mrs. Van Dorn added, "They are beautiful and tucked in on the bend of the lane. It's almost as if they wanted their privacy from the main roads and harbor hubbub. However, they needed access to the shops and harbor."

"I wonder if either has tunnels underneath, especially to the wharf?"

"That's an interesting thought?" Mr. Van Dorn remarked.

"Why not? They built tunnels from some of the grand homes to the James River. There are some historical accounts that Mr. Shaw may have helped build one of those homes. He used similar shipbuilding techniques for joist bracing and bracing. The same man worked on the wooden cabinets, which shows the hand of a highly skilled artisan."

"I suspect Luke Shaw's touch of shipbuilding gave it the majestic bones to help it last all these years," added Mrs. Fitz.

"The two homes in Charleston are both lovely homes and appeared well taken care of all these years. However, I'm not sure if he had any hand in their construction." Mr. Van Dorn added. "The homeowners provided me with no new information."

"So, you have once belonged to Thomas Hill. That's remarkable. It leads credence to the rumor that Luke Shaw did not die at sea after a battle with an English Frigate along the coast. Hmm. It suggests he at least left a family if the man passed his belongings on."

"That was what our family always believed:" Mr. Fitz added. "Our family never felt he died in that so-called fight at sea. Instead, I believe he was the captain that survived. The completed painting was done in the late 1780s or early 1790s, which would have been after Captains Shaw or Hawke died. He reportedly had died at sea.

Oral tradition says. Kitty Van Dorn painted it. Something doesn't fit in the story."

Matt chimed in. "Let me show you the original painting. I have a magnifying glass to take a better look at the signature."

"Wow! The painting is the portrait of Captain Hill. I've heard about it." Mrs. Van Dorn said with excitement. "He was a very handsome man, even with age," she stated as she sat back and appreciated the painting.

Mr. Van Dorn picked up the magnifier to look closer at the initials. "The initials read K. H. It could be for Kitty Hill?"

"Yes, he was handsome," Angie whispered as she looked at Matt. "I'm a believer. She wouldn't have painted this man if he had been a pirate or a scoundrel." She looked at the strokes of the shadings of his frock and face. "Someone who respected and adored the subject made these strokes. She may not have been as skilled as an Audubon or a Renoir, but you feel the passion for the subject. That's not hatred. It has more depth than a professional painter would have done then. They may have had more skills with the lines and color palette, but this hand had emotion when she made the strokes."

"How do you pick up on these things, Angie?" Matt asked.

"That's what I do with historic preservation. So, I have an eye for these things like that," Angie responded.

"I have other news that I received this weekend. This information has not been verified yet or documented. I am hesitant to say much more until that is completed." Matt paused. "There are signs of a shipwreck on the coast near an island south of here. I'm not going to give you the location yet. There are some visual clues that it was a British Frigate. I don't think it left much to tell a story about in detail. What bothers me is that I don't think it should have been there. Damage may have occurred by a storm or anchored for repair, but my source says it looks like it had taken a beating before it went down. It makes me curious. That's all I'm going to say." Matt stated. "It fits a possibility from oral traditions.

But I don't know."

"Do you have plans to dive into it?" Matt's dad asked.

"Yes, I would like the state authorities to permit us to use it as a maritime research site if possible. That would allow us to use technology to document the site more carefully."

"I think that's fantastic," Mr. Van Dorn added.

"I'm going to let you all look at the things in the box," Matt said. He turned to the soft bundle he had in his arms. "Angie, is there anything else you would like to ask?"

She laid her head again on Matt's chest. "No."

"Well, that settles that. I will wake up the other fur ball beside my feet and take Sam outside. Angie, you may join me if you please." Angie took the cue and went with Matt to the backyard.

"You look tired. Are you sure you want to drive back to Charleston tonight?" Matt asked.

“Yeah, I’ll be fine. I might brew some fresh coffee first. It’s been a long weekend. I’ll enjoy having some time by myself. Tomorrow is light. I will sleep in and work from home. The work will get done. I’ll get out and take a walk when I need some fresh air.” Angie said.

“I don’t like you having to drive back and forth. We’ll work out everything else,” Matt replied.

“It’s fine. Your diving, is it dangerous?” Angie asked.

“It can be,” Matt responded.

“Would you ever stop for me?” Angie asked. “I doubt it. I guess it depends on the reason. Why?”

“He did it for her, you know?” Angie stated.

“What are you talking about?” Matt asked.

“Captain Bodacious loved her so much that he wanted to make the choices he did,” Angie replied.

“What?” Matt responded, seeking clarification.

“Savannah and Charleston were only ports to Captain Hill. These cities were not his home. He came here because Kitty was removed and placed away from her family after being forced to marry Captain Hawke. Find the date when the Frigate went down. See if the houses were built the houses shortly after that date. Also, check to see if the stories of Captain Bodacious stop. Kitty’s father helped build the two homes for his daughters in Charleston. Also, see if you can find out if the beams match a shipbuilder’s style of building a ship's hull. There is evidence of that happening in a home along one of Virginia's rivers. That house had a tunnel built. Remember, I have studied historical architecture." Angie said.

"I see you were paying attention in class. Was the professor good-looking?" Matt teased.

"You are impossible. The instructor was attractive, and we went out for coffee once."

"I rest my case. Go on. I'm listening." Matt replied, enjoying Angie's passion for something they had in common.

Angie narrowed her eyes at Matt and then went back to her story. "The other sister was Katherine. She died in childbirth. Kitty eventually raised the child as her own. I would assume his father couldn't care for the child because of his occupation or illness. However, the relationship became legal after the child's father passed on and Kitty remarried her second husband. That male child was not a Hawke. His name was Fitz. The child carried the paternal name of his biological father, who died shortly after his wife. The child's first name was Charles Fitz. Kitty and her second husband, Captain Thomas Hill, lived comfortably. They eventually sold the home in Charleston a few years later and moved away. The painting you have most likely came from Charles Fitz's family heirlooms. One would be led to believe the painting you have is of Captain Hill. There are no known descriptions of Captain Thomas Hill prior to 1777. I am most certain it's the only one made. That was a family heirloom, never to be outside of the family, according to the will. It was part of Charles Fitz's inheritance when his adoptive parents passed. Interesting stories are part of Captain Hill's legacy. He served in the Continental militia and, later, the navy. He was given a captain's pension. More interesting is that Captain Hawke died at sea and his widow marries soon after."

"How do you know all this?" Matt asked.

"I do my research, too. Except I was researching the two sister's house. I can connect the dots my father was looking for. I haven't even told him yet," Angie responded.

"All this pouting you've been doing about the elephant in the room has been a farce. You've known the missing piece all along."

"Maybe, most of it. But it's good to make you all fess up after leaving me out of the circle." Angie replied.

"You're good, and I can see I'm over my head. But life with you will never be boring, will it?"

"Probably not," Angie said and kissed him. "I need to get back, though. Let me tell our folks good night and let me drive on back."
"Okay, but don't make me wait too long." He put his cheek against her silky hair. "I'm still waiting on the bomb."

Angie laughed and pushed him gently away so she could begin her walk back into the house. Finally, it was time to say goodbye to everyone.

Chapter 14

THE FIRST THING Matt did on Monday morning was to arrange a dive with some friends on staff with the University's Marine Ecology program. Revisiting the site again was his goal. He now believed there was an actual shipwreck, and it was within twelve miles of the U.S. jurisdiction. The ship should at least be documented if it existed. As for finding anything of archeology worth, he had his doubts. There was nothing brazenly obvious when he was in the area a few weeks back, but usually, there isn't unless you know what you are looking for on the sea bottom. As for the bad guys that Bitters talked about, Matt wasn't sure who that might be. If there was any genuine treasure, he was certain that someone would have discovered it before now. That didn't appear to be the case with his research on permits, sightings, and lists of known wreckages. Maybe there was something different about this site that made it less identifiable. It was worth exploring, even if nothing came from it. Getting permits should be easy with the

University team's help. Matt also wanted to research what may have been around the shoreline then. *Was there something that might draw a British Frigate to the area around that period?* Matt couldn't think of anything off the top of his head, but maybe there was something unknown.

Monday was filled with client visits as well. The routine work on the land was still a part of his work from day to day. By the end of what he had, he was feeling done in. He was sure Angie would feel the same, so he tried not to bother her. However, he sent her several texts to let her know he was thinking about her. She'd answered back with a short line. Matt would fix the mileage between them if the engagement dragged out too long. He enjoyed her company and missed her when they weren't together. A short-term problem, he thought to himself.

Angie dragged a bit on Monday. She made it to class on time but failed to remember anything discussed. Angie girded herself with a cup of coffee before meeting in the conference room at work for the weekly meeting. Since most people were at the gathering the day before, she felt she was in understanding company. The team reviewed deadlines and progressed to current stories being explored for the fall magazine. I think we are on target with everything. We have a new advertiser for the coveted last page, thanks to Stanley. Can we add an article about a healthcare worker and work it up to help them with a recruiting need? Follow up with the H.R. department and see their most important recruiting needs. Maybe we could add something to that area. The University has a lot of medical programs, and we could highlight an alum or a program.

How about a search and rescue operation at sea or in the harbor? Indeed, we have some alum connections in that area. We could do an article on medical treatment or emergency planning when there is a ship accident like the one we just had. If the fall is tied up, we could save it for the winter to spring magazines.

"I like the idea, Angie. Maybe you could own that one. I'd like to see what you put together," the editor said. "It's not like we can't do both healthcare-related stories. That's a critical job sector in this town."

After the meeting broke up, Lauren ran over to catch Angie's elbow as they moved to their cubicles. "So, when are you thinking of planning the wedding?" Lauren asked.

"I don't know. I haven't thought about it. Things have been so hectic; my mind can only do so much.?"

Lauren smiled back. "I am here to help if you need someone."

"Thanks. Hey, and thanks for coming down yesterday too. I hope you had fun," Angie said.

"Of course I did. So did Jarl. I've never been to an engagement party where people meshed and did things together. I'm used to sitting around tables being polite or standing guard at the buffet table. It was fun to get down a little dirty for a change. When you mother called and said T-shirts and sneakers were desired, I was all in."

"That's Matt's mother's forte. She is very gifted with event planning and entertainment. My parents are fairly good at that sort of thing, too. So, I guess Matt and I grew up with similar parents in that regard. We were always ourselves with people. We had people that seemed to hang out with us, even if it was to watch a football game on the television." Angie laughed, remembering an old memory about her father. "Pageant nights were the annual event my father planned to escape. He knew it would be nothing but girls talking and giggling all night. My father declared some important appointment he had, like bowling night with his friends. Mother couldn't clear off the table fast enough before Dad was out of the house."

"They sound like great parents," Lauren said.

"They were. I liked up there." Angie said as she finished her coffee and put it in the basket.

"Maybe that's what Matt likes about you. He sees your happiness," Lauren added.

"I hope so. Matt's teaching me things about myself I never really paid attention to until now."

"He sounds like a winner, and I'm glad you both met. Now, I am off to decorate an orange room for one of those houses along the river. I will be envious while there, showing the owner some of my suggestions. I could put a brown burlap sack in that room, and it would still look divine."

"Hey, that sounds like fun. Your ideas, I'm sure, will be stunning. See you later." Thirty minutes later, Angie left the office as well. She walked a few blocks and then picked up the trolley to the historic district. Daydreaming, Angie missed her stop closest to the apartment and ended up getting off three blocks down where the cluster of churches was. One of these churches was where she picked up her parents after the incident with the cruise liner. Angie stepped off the trolley, followed the sidewalk past the first, and read the historical marker, checking out when it had been built. After passing the second church, she walked through the wrought-iron gate and around the gravesites. Other pedestrians had also wandered in, passing respectfully by the markers of those centuries before. The children's markers were the ones that tugged at the heart the most. Their lives were from a different era. Death was not an uncommon presence in the lives of the colonists.

As she circled the path, she saw two old markers side by side. Though some intricate details had worn off, the names could still be seen. General Caleb Fitz was a Beloved father and husband. December 17, 1743- June 16, 1777. A marker showed it was a grave for an American revolutionary war veteran. Angie took a photo to show Matt. Beside his tombstone was another with the name Katherine Fitz. The etchings were challenging to read, but it looked like March 7, 1753—September 3, 1777. They died almost months apart. Angie knew the records showed the two houses were built between 1776 and 1778. Captain Hawke died at sea reportedly on September 17, 1777. The timeline fit. If her suspicions were correct,

Kitty Van Dorn's second husband, Captain Thomas Hill, must have previously known each other. The parents may have baptized their child at this church since the graves are here. Angie wondered if the baptismal registry went back that far. After looking at the other names, she circled inside the church and met a lovely woman. Angie spoke with her for some time and left, feeling more excited than when she arrived.

Several hours later, she was lying across the bed with the bunny at her fingertips and the phone near the pillow.

"I met a delightful woman today while I was out today. She was such a darling. We spent a long time talking about a lot of things. She had much to share about all kinds of things I'm interested in. The woman grew up in France, knew about fabrics, French cooking, music, and design. She also gave me a clue on where I might find something."

"I wish I was there to see your face light up about all those things you love. Do you like classical music?" Matt asked.

"Yes, I do. I have had singing lessons for several years, and I also play the violin, harp, and piano."

"I'm impressed "

"Unfortunately, I have few connections here to use what I know."

"I bet you have a lot more talents that I want to find out about."

"Yes. But back to my interesting discovery today." Angie continued.

"I'm listening," Matt said.

"I found the graves of Thomas Fitz and his wife Katherine in the church, where I met the nice docent."

"That's interesting. You'll have to show me when I come up next weekend."

"Promise?" Angie said with enthusiasm.

"Wow, those words sound as if you missed me." Matt teased.

"I did. I missed you a lot! But I can be happy when you're not here. I'm happier when you are with me wherever we are."

"So, have you made any significant purchases lately? I'm thinking of something white, but I'm negotiable if you'd like something nontraditional. My preference is a little shoulder showing because I love messaging those shoulders," Matt teased.

"There's been no time to think about it since I got back. But I know I want to keep things simple. I might pick something up in New York, an Haute couture number. If Lauren and I go shopping, you can bet it will have a lot of lace. I will stop her when she gets too close to the Cinderella dresses."

"I'm game for whatever you pick out. However, I would prefer that you pick out something soon. I'm not that patient. If you mess with me too long, I might drag you off in cutoff jeans and a t-shirt and do a jump over the broom for our vows."

"That won't do at all. I'm thinking of the chapel at the academy in the fall with the leaves changing. You are a graduate, and both parents are former instructors. Surely, we would be allowed."

"Yes, we could do that. I don't think the shorts idea would fare too well with the dress code. But our parents would probably love the idea."

"Would it be strange not to have a real reception, but more like a sending away gathering so we could leave the chapel, get dressed for travel, and be sent off by our family?"

"I like it. Your mother and my mother are so good with things like that. I bet you could produce something that would be great. Just make it soon. That's all I ask."

"So, while I'm shopping for the killer dress, what are you doing this weekend?"

"I'm going to be diving this weekend down near my parents. I've organized a marine archeologist and another diver with a team up top to document a potential shipwreck site. We'll see if it is or not. I don't know which way it will go."

"That sounds exciting!" Ange replied.

Matt continued. "Probably not, but maybe. It's what I like to do. I've been trained to do this, so it's in my blood."

"I'm very fortunate to have someone in my life that is not boring, despite what those bow ties you wear would suggest."

Matt smiled back. "Say what you will, but I think they make a statement."

"Yes, I do too, babe. But I'm glad it's bow ties and not tight, straight-leg jeans with cowboy boots. Otherwise, I'm afraid I would have to fend everyone off."

"Growl," Matt added to teased. "Well, it's getting late, and I know you need to sleep. So, I will say good night. I wanted you to know that Sam and I miss you."

"I'll call you in a few days. Bye." Matt touched a button on his phone and scrolled through the pictures until he found the one he had made of her at the harbor. Don't leave me, sweet angel. He touched her face and let the screen saver turn off.

"That is sweet," said Angie to herself. She smiled and pressed the off button. She picked up the bunny and put it back in the box for the night. "Yes, cutie, let's get some sleep and let tomorrow come. Then there will be one less day until we are all together."

The rest of the week for both went smoothly. However, the weekend together would have to wait till next weekend.

Matt planned a dive this weekend. Angie was set on working on her project for school and maybe a little recreation riding her bike. Angie needed the quiet time to appreciate what was changing on the inside.

Chapter 15

SATURDAY FINALLY ARIVED. Matt headed out early to the marina, where he caught up with the team.

"It's a little choppy out here today, but we should be okay," said the pilot.

"We'll just take a peek and see what's done there. If there's anything, we'll gather some photos and data, and if not, we've had a great swim, right?" said the man sitting across from Matt on the boat.

"You got it," Matt replied.

Dr. Santoro took a thorough look at the terrain. "I'm looking at the shoreline. Even today, there's not much built on the far shoreline where the continent begins. The nature preserve protects the island. There're a lot of marshes in the northern half. The south shore has a bit of a bluff that someone could have built on or farmed. I don't know if there would be any remains there or not.

The only way to reach it is by sea. Perfect for pirating, except it's a little more exposed to storms out here as a barrier island. Pirates typically used inlets and protected coves to create their sanctuaries away from other passing enemies. I don't know of any rocks or other water obstructions that would cause a shipwreck. The maritime forest would have extended much further into the water than today, so maybe the spot is closer to land than it looks now. We'd have to estimate how much erosion has occurred on the shoreline over the last three hundred years. It's all fascinating. Let's go for it!"

With everyone ready. The divers each took their steps off the boat hosting this exploration today. A robot with a camera was also used to explore the site so that it could be documented and filed with the appropriate governmental agencies.

The divers were in the slightly shallower ground, diving about two thousand feet deep. Fish of different hues passed around them. Other creatures scurried without paying attention to the divers. On the surface of the seabed, the terrain was sandy with bumps here and there. A few yards in front, protrusions from the sea bottom were noted. Each of the divers moved in that direction. What appeared to be a ship's hull measuring large enough to be a frigate was stressed. Encrustations were noted growing on what would seem like a debris field. A long rock-like formation appeared to be the length of a cannon from a ship. Time would run out on this first attempt to explore the wreckage, but proof that the wreckage existed was worth it all. Other dives would be scheduled to explore this site further now that it was found. Matt tried his best to look for something that could identify the ship that he could bring up on this first attempt. Again, time was running out. One last look to the right before preparing for the ascent. He moved his hands again, hoping to clear away the sandy bottom of something appearing metal like a coating of encrustation. Matt was becoming more animated with his hands to the other divers. He began taking shots of something on the seabed and of his watch to mark the spot. He was running out of time, but he knew that's what he needed to see.

"Base to divers. Time to surface."

"Roger that, diver 1," Dr. Santoro said. He then signaled to the other divers, and the ascent for returning to the surface was underway.

Once all aboard, the high fives went around the group. "That is a find. We'll let those guys on the second team take another look to see if they can add more information. After that, we'll get the grid ready and start working. On the site. I think that was a British Frigate, given what appeared to be the size of the hull."

Matt added, "If that's a bell I found down there and it has a name on it, I bet it's The Constellation."

"Why do you think that?" Dr. Santoro asked.

"Lucky guess. I think I read the story." Matt shrugged his shoulders and relaxed on the bench. He felt the peace of knowing his mission was done for the day. Tomorrow will bring a set of directions.

That evening, he sat up for a while with his dad playing a game of chess. He paused for several seconds before making his next move.

"What's on your mind about the future, Matt?"

"I don't know, Dad," Matt replied. "Things are moving fast right now. I told Angie I didn't want to wait very long. She was thinking about setting the date in the fall and having the wedding at the chapel at the academy. I thought that was fine. Given her dad's and your history and my graduating there, I thought that was a neat idea. But maybe it would be better to pick something different. I will leave that to the women in the family. I'll be wherever they tell me to be."

"That's a pretty good rule of thumb when you are working around women," his dad teased with his dry humor. "But, of course, Charleston is a bigger town; it might have more opportunities for both of you. Have you thought of that?"

"You may be right. Maybe we'll move out west and have a ranch. I'll learn how to rope cows, and Angie will learn to ride horses."

"Well, that would be harder on your mother and me, but we could try driving the chuck wagon to all the grandkids' horse shows. She's a wonderful cook. I'm sure she could make a good pot of chili for everybody."

"Dad, now you've gone too far. I can't see you or Mother in a pair of chaps."

"Don't know. It could be a lot of fun. A man could find much space for a man's cave on one of those ranches—stars in the sky and sleeping on the ground cowboy style."

"Dad, be real. Passed are your days of sleeping on the ground without a goose-feathered comforter and full body-size pillow. Mother has gotten you spoiled, and you know it. Checkmate!"

"Well, isn't that something? I know my son has gotten too smart for his own good when he beats his old man at chess." The elder Fitz patted his son on the shoulder and started out to the kitchen to fill his mug.

"Dad, I've been able to beat you for years. I've just let you win, so I can still get a free meal and a bed from my parents occasionally.

"You're just like me, son, always thinking and never showing your hand," Matt's dad replied.

The following day, Matt went out to meet again with Dr. Santoro and the rest of the crew. After finding the site and preparing the equipment, Matt was ready to take another dive. This time, they were prepared to remove some more substantial items from the site and take them back as part of its artifacts. They need to decide if they can be removed without destruction. That was always the dilemma when excavating a site. Matt was reluctant to disturb the area; perhaps secrets were better left unknown.

The tedious work began. After thirty minutes, another team of divers went down to continue the work for today. Matt waited on board, helping with communication, and logging the information after his first dive. After today, he would return to his work on land. There may be opportunities to dive into the site again with the team, but he also knew he had to allocate some time in Charleston. The team could take it from here. If there was something particularly technical, they would contact him. By noon, the artifact Matt was most interested in came up in the reinforced fiber netting that could lift several hundreds of pounds.

The encrusted object looked like a large glob of rough-covered shells and plant life. It would be taken back to the lab, where it would be gently cleaned.

Matt knew without cleaning the object what it was. It was proof that determined the last spot of Captain Hawke on that fateful day in September. *However, who was the bad guy, and the good had yet to be determined?*

Chapter 16

ANGIE HAD SPENT a pleasant weekend staying in town. She ran first thing in the morning to start the weekend. Angie had missed this part of her past routine. She checked her phone for texts. None from the one she wanted. She was a little disappointed. However, she kept herself busy. Angie made good on her promise to wash her car. She then rinsed her patio and let the cool water from the hose pour over her before she went inside to get out of the humidity. After freshening up and putting on her favorite fragrance and sundress, Angie went about town. Maybe she could window shop down on the main street. Stanley had texted and mentioned that he was playing a game of softball tomorrow with a pickup team, and they needed some players. He asked if she wanted to join them. Angie said, "Yes." So, on Sunday, Stanley picked her up in his old pickup around 1:00 PM. Bats, gloves, and a cooler filled the back of the truck bed. Only minor grass stains on her white sneakers and dirt from her bottom from taking a spill at the home plate were noted as significant changes. Her naturally blond hair was still in a ponytail underneath a white cap with only a few strands hanging loose.

"It's not my business. But I hope your lawyer's fiancé doesn't change you too much. I kind of like you the way you are. You fit in with the team well. We'd hate to lose you as our backup bat girl." Stanley teased.

"You can bet on the former. As for the backup role, I was considering applying for the promotion of plate duster."

Stanley looked over. "No, that's for the referee, and you cheat too much for that position.

"Hey, the girl's got to win one way or another! It was a lot of fun, and I'm glad I accepted. It was a friendly group of people.

"Yeah, they are pretty good folks. All with their quirks, of course, but when you need help, you can count on one of them to come through. So why didn't your girlfriend come today?"

"Charlotte was with her sister doing a baby shower thing. She volunteered your name. She knew I was safe with you, being engaged to Mr. Wonderful."

"Safe!" Angie responded. Agitation was stirring in her mind, but she paused momentarily to think. "Well, maybe she's right. However, I want you to know I appreciated you asking me, and

Matt wouldn't have been jealous that way. He would want me to have fun and enjoy life."

"Sounds like you got a good one. This guy has a job, likes dogs, and pays for dinner when he asks you out. Not too many of us southern gentlemen left," Stanley replied.

"Wait, he's not from here originally." Angie remarked.

"I rest my case."

"Stanley, you are one of a kind!" Angie replied with a smile.

"Yep, that's me." Stanley had fun teased his passenger. However, the rest of the drive home was less chatty as both ran out of fuel. The heat and humidity of the day wiped away their energy for nothing but going home.

When Angie returned home, she returned Matt's call. It was after 8:00 PM and she was delighted to hear his voice on the phone, not his voicemail. "I know it's late. It's the first time I've had to return your call. There is so much to do here!"

Matt heard the excitement in her voice. "My dad and I were talking about that this weekend. Have you considered where you would like to live once we are married?"

"Oh, not really. I assumed I would be wherever you were."
"Would you be happy in a small town?" Matt asked.

"Well, if I had a choice," Angie paused for a few seconds. "Um, I don't want to commit to an answer to that question yet."

"That's fair enough for this evening, but I want you to think hard about that question."

Angie responded, "Okay, I will think about it. Did you mention anything about the chapel to your parents?"

"Yes, I did. My folks liked the idea, but they'll agree to anything we want.

"Okay, I'll work on that this week and see if there are any roadblocks to that idea. I can think of one. I want you to give me an honest answer."

"Okay, shoot."

Angie hesitated. "Will it remind you of your first fiancé?" she asked.

"That's a fair question. Dad asked the same thing. I hadn't thought about it when you mentioned it. But you're the second individual that has said something. I don't want our day to be infused with someone else's ghost."

"I agree." Angie responded. "That means I'm going to select another place that is beautiful and happy. I promise we'll find a location that is unique to our special day."

"I'm for that. There's a chapel in Vegas we could think about," Matt teased.

"No! I had a layover there once at midnight. It was the loudest neon-lit place I've ever seen!" Angie replied.

"Yeah! Great nightlife, though! Too bad it was only a layover." Matt continued to tease.

"I'm not belittling it. It's just not for my wedding or honeymoon! So, take that off your list of likes!" Angie answered with amusement.

"Oh well, I must accept the choice of some bucolic pasture instead. You with daisies in your hair and bare feet. I will have shirtless attire and bell bottom jeans, saying our vows in front of the lambs and goats."

"It could work as long as the cows are not too pesky!" Matt continued to teased.

"Stop! I will find a place that is a winner for both of us."

"Pick up another outfit at that shop on the main street and set the date with a time. I promise to say my sacred promise anywhere after that."

"You are so cute when you are being silly. New topic. What do we know about your dive this weekend?"

"The marine archeologists are still exploring and making a site grid. There was one thing I showed them that appeared to be something I was very interested in. I wanted them to go back and see if they could lift it to the surface for further analysis. The second team may have pulled it out as part of excavating the area of materials that were significant and unique to the wreckage. It would identify the ship's name and give us more information on why it was there and what may be part of the debris. The archeologist said it might be interesting to investigate the areas on the shoreline to see if the return fire was coming from land or sea. It's a guessing game of who was chasing who. All we have is the one that went down. It looks like a fight, not a storm or obstruction, doomed the ship. My gut feeling is that it wasn't pirates. The debris field was too large. Maybe I'm wrong. I will let the experts figure it out." Matt was momentarily quiet and then blurted out, "Angie, you're wonderful! Do you know you just made me think of something? I am going to email Dr. Santoro tonight. The direction of the cannons. That's brilliant!"

"What did I say about cannons?" Angie asked rhetorically.

"That's the clue. The cannons were aimed at something. That's the last thing they were ordered to do. I'm not sure that's what brought them down. We'll have to get some more information. Maybe we won't ever know. Something else unexpected happened today. The pilot on the yacht that hit the ship died of a heart attack this morning. It made the evening news."

"That's sad," Angie said.

"I'm sure the weekend took a toll on him. They interviewed him extensively, I am sure. Maybe the stress of what happened got to him. He wasn't that young of a man and had many things going on. I don't think he took good care of himself, either. He lived a hard life. But he was a diligent worker. One could never say he was a slouch. He made decisions that made his life hard and was given a tough hand. I'm not sure which came first."

"Did you know him well?" Angie asked.

"No. He was someone around town that people knew. He had been a client."

"Well, I'm sorry for him and everyone else who was injured."

"I don't think many injuries, and none were threatening from what I heard. It was an odd deal. Perhaps the yacht had some nefarious activity on board. That's for the investigators to figure out. I'm glad your parents were not hurt. Despite the event on the cruise liner, I think they enjoyed themselves. Before that happened, they had a wonderful time, they said. I am glad I was close enough to bring them to my place, so they could destress from all that happened."

"Of course they did. They were thrilled to meet up again with you and your parents. They love being near the ocean, although Dad would be just as comfortable in a lawn chair with an enjoyable book anywhere. Being in advertising all those years, you'd think he would be more like a go-happy guy. Instead, he has his cerebral side. Mother is all fun, completely my dad's opposite."

"Yes, I like that about her. I like both of your parents."

Angie responded, "That is good because they will be your in-laws and want to treat you like their son. Luckily enough, that is a good thing."

"Mm, I like that too. But, you know, I always have to say this, but it's getting late, and I know you need your sleep."

"Yeah, all right, I'll let you say goodnight. But I want to hear that you're planning to come here this weekend," Angie stated.

"That is the plan. I will call you before Friday. Goodnight."

"Good night," Angie responded. She plopped back on her pillow. Within a few minutes, she was fast asleep.

Chapter 17

MATT NOTED HIS entire morning was full of clients when he opened his calendar the following day. He didn't have time to check emails or texts between the morning office visits. He skipped lunch and grabbed a green beverage from the office refrigerator between 1:00 and 2:00 appointments. By three 3:30 PM, he spotted a message he was looking for. He sat back in his chair and peeked at the email. There it was, the photo. Matt's anticipation was finally soothed. He could read the words Constellation embedded in the metal in print. Matt's mind churned out ideas about the scenario of the last day of Captain Hawke and his ship. *The team had the bell in their possession. What else would be found in the debris field, or would the remains remain secret to only the sea gods and goddesses?* The British could claim its contents. Matt had no desire to attach any ownership of its history. The question remained of what brought it down. *Was the story true that persisted today? The jealous Captain Hawke lost his life and his ship and affected the war's outcome by chasing a ghost known as Captain Bodacious.*

Matt went to the internet and ordered some reference books that were still available. He then emailed a couple of questions to Dr. Santoro. That was all Matt had time for today on the issue. He left the office after the last client. There were a few errands around town that he wanted to complete before the end of the day. He had promised a friend he'd meet at his place at 7:00 PM. Something was rattling on a motorcycle that Matt was supposed to know something about. Matt was thrilled to check out what was happening. He had one just like it before he went to college.

By mid-week, Matt was already looking forward to the weekend. He had debated about planning something or letting things happen. Matt laughed to himself. Before he met Angie, there was a plan for everything. Matt had a plan for everything. But, since she came into his life, he has learned that spontaneity has its benefits too.

Angie's voice decided for him when he heard her excitement over the phone.

"Matt, I found the dress! I found it in a store today in Charleston. It's a long story. I will tell you most of it on Saturday. But I must ask for a favor. The owner asked my two friends and me to come over for tea on Saturday, and I can try on the dress at her home."

"That's weird!" Matt said.

"No, it's not! The owner is the woman I met at church when I found the grave sites. Remember, we talked for a long time? We talked about my love for music and if I would like to play for the choir. Remember? Guess where she lives?"

"I don't know. In the church bell tower?"

"No! She lives in Kitty Van Dorn's home. Michelle's husband is a shipping executive. If Dad had previously talked to her to find information about the family, perhaps he didn't know what to ask, or she was afraid to divulge information to a stranger.? However, she was happy to talk to me about her house. Maybe she made the connection."

"Now that is interesting. That's spooky and interesting. Does the woman seem normal?"

"Absolutely! The dress is one of a kind. It was made for someone else, but the bride became pregnant and was too far along to get into the dress by the wedding time. The alterations would have ruined the dress, so the shop devised a backup solution for her and kept the dress to resell. It's never been worn."

"If you like it, that's all that matters. Back to the lady with the house. How did you get invited for tea?"

"I asked if she could hold the dress until I could bring my two friends by the shop tomorrow. I put a deposit on it to show my earnestness. It wouldn't be fun picking out my dress alone. I wanted somebody there with me to celebrate. That's when she said that she would take the dress home and that my friends and I could come over for tea on Saturday and try it on. She said she had a studio in her house and could pin it if any alterations were needed. In her younger days, she worked in France at one of the famous designer houses. That's where she met her husband, in France. He moved up in the company and was eventually given a position in the North American division based in Charleston. He was raised in the Tidewater area in Virginia. She doesn't design anymore now that she is older. However, she told me she dabbles occasionally. I told you this was a long story. You can hear the rest of it this weekend."

"Do you still want me to come?" Matt asked.

"Yes, but would you like to come later after I come home? Or would you like to come up as planned and hang out until I'd be gone for just a couple of hours?"

"We'll see. I will come up. I'll check my schedule and see what works best since you'll be with friends. It sounds like a fun time, just weird. Do I have to wonder what is bringing all these events together? You'll have to tell me all about the house. I'm sure it has been modernized over the centuries. Wonder if they have any stories of their own to tell."

"For certain, I will make notes of what Mrs. Duvall says. I can't wait and I can't believe I found the dress without even trying. Now we can move to the next step and find a place and a date."

"Be sensitive to the southern football conference playoff dates—a bad day for any events that include men. I'm not one of those guys that do not have a favorite team, but I have friends that invite me to their favorite team's playoffs. Let's not make me choose between my wedding day and the playoff game of the century."

"I promise!" Angie responded.

"Thank you. Wow, that settles what most newlyweds fight over in their first year of marriage. I think we're doing pretty well so far. I can't wait to be with you. It feels like it's been a very long time since I've been able to touch your hand or smell your hair. Do we have to do anything special? I could enjoy just walking with you at sunset and eating in. Maybe we could ride our bikes on the beach at sunrise on Sunday. I would like that."

"I would like all of that, too," said Angie.

"Maybe I will pop down to Dad's and Mom's next week to check out an area about which I've been thinking. I'd take you too, but I don't know what kind of terrain it is. It may be wild. I might ask one of my diving friends to come. We are always looking for an adventure."

"I'm looking forward to a shoulder rub when you come." Angie teased.

"Now, that wish might get me a speeding ticket."

"I'll see you on Saturday. Goodnight."

"Okay, goodnight," Angie said. She went outside on the patio and looked up at the stars. God, I don't think it's so weird. You've always been in control of my life. It gets weird and messed up when I take control back.

Matt followed up on his plan for the week. According to his friend Jake, no significant news came from the shipwreck in sight. It takes a long time to map and document. According to Ian, most of the ship had been destroyed before it went under, which Matt also felt. His research did not show that the Constellation was with a fleet of ships during this time. Mat wrote some thoughts and questions in notes that he could go back and review later. He then recorded his thoughts so he could hear his ideas later. *What was it doing alone?* Matt put a question mark by the Caribbean. He could have been heading for the Caribbean to find men to crew the boat. Matt had discovered that pirates and unscrupulous captains found men to operate a ship in any way they could. Savannah has many old tales of mysterious things happening along its riverfront, where the wharfs and taverns saw the stew pot of humanity. Matt's research showed Captain Hawke's commitment to the British Navy was that he provided his own ship. And his wealthy family had paid for his commission as an officer. Matt thought *Captain Hawke sounded more like a privateer. From what he had found out he was possibly more of a pirate than his enemy, Captain B.* Literature showed that pirates would not normally use a frigate because of the slower speed. The known advantage is that it could haul more. It was a military ship, so the Constellation would be expected to have a larger crew, supplies, and cannons., It could have been products like cotton or international goods that required more supplies for longer journeys. Whatever Captain Hawke was, he liked to present himself as an officer of the British Realm and use that to his advantage. Someone witnessed that ship going down that September and noted that

Captain Hawkes died that day. It was assumed he died on the ship. Is that the way it all went down? The records Matt could find so far were rather sketchy on who saw what and how. *Maybe they'll find something in the wreckage to reveal its mission. The ship had gone down in this location and was being noticed after all this time. Why didn't the ship have a beginning or an endpoint? Did any documents on what happened exist?*

By Friday, Matt was ready to end the week. He talked with Angie and was going to drive up Saturday afternoon. She would leave a key for him, and Matt and Sam could relax and enjoy the place. She would keep the bunny in the crate until she got back, and they could introduce Sam to Bella together under close supervision.

Chapter 18

"THANK YOU, SO much for having us here today. Your invitation was more than what I could ever expect." Angie responded.

"Please, I will have as much fun as you girls. Now let's try on the dress before we have tea. That way, you won't feel bloated in the dress.

"I have it back here. Follow me. Michelle showed them to a sunny room that looked over the courtyard. I demanded this room when we bought this home. My husband had to take a room that looked at the drive lined with azaleas and hostas. At least it is the cooler of the rooms because that side of the house is shaded. I had to have my sunshine. I will draw the drapes a bit so one can peek in. Go into that room right there, Angie, and try it on. When you are ready, come on out. These large mirrors should help you see nearly all the way around." Michelle said.

"Charlotte and Lauren, we must find something for you when you're ready. It won't be too long with two pretty girls like you. When I was young, I had so many boys coming around my parents' home that they had to make a rule that they could only stay for an hour and never on Sundays. When I reached eighteen, they could stay as long as I wanted. My parents grew up in an older generation and were very strict about dating. But those were beautiful years. Then I went off to Paris and studied fashion. I was always good at sewing. My mother had taught me that, but when I learned how to design and use fabrics in all kinds of ways, which was what I loved the most.

"Oh, my goodness. The dress is gorgeous." Angie said, holding back tears.

"Ahh, she has it on. Come on out and let us see!" Michelle said.

Angie walked out of the dress. It was the first wedding dress she had ever tried on, and she didn't want to try another.

"Only princesses look this beautiful!" Lauren said.

"Wow!" Charlotte added. "That dress will knock Matt on his behind."

Angie kept smiling. "It's beautiful, and it doesn't need much down. Do you think this will be okay for a fall wedding? I don't want to change anything.

Michelle spoke up. "I don't think you should. We can make a little cape when moving from outside to inside. But once you are inside, it is beautiful like it is. I suggest adding something that makes it your dress only. Let me think. Do you have a necklace that is a family heirloom?"

"My mother might have something. I have a small diamond stud I could wear." Angie said.

"Mm, well, that might work. You will know when it gets closer time. Things like that seem to call one's name. It should be a piece that symbolizes the qualities that make you beautiful in this man's eyes. For every woman, it's something unique. That's the piece you will wear!"

"I like that idea," Angie said. Looking in the mirror, she admired the details of the gown. "It's so pretty. I don't want to take it off."

"That's what it should do. But go ahead, and I will wrap it back up. I will return it to the shop and prepare it for your day. It will be perfect. Now let's have some refreshments. I have something delightful right over here to try." She led them to a sun porch off the studio. There was a small table with some sweat. On a tray with wheels was some lemon, iced tea, and round paper lace doilies for coasters.

"Let's enjoy this pretty day," the dress shop owner said. "This house is well suited for entertaining small garden parties and dinners with friends. Kyle and I thought this was a perfect house for that, and we love it, but parking is such an issue. If we have a large house party, we must plan a shuttle from somewhere, which is a bother. But it solves the problem. Old houses have such character."

"Yes, I admired this house and the neighbors the first time I walked down this street," Angie said.

"Yes, it has that appeal," Michelle responded. "I'll show you around before you go. So, girls, what makes you love living here in Charleston when young people could be in so many places?"

"Well, I was born in the area," said Lauren. "I like my family close by. I always do stuff with my sisters or go to Mom and Dad's place."

"I'm sure your parents love having you near, too. Family is so wonderful to have around you. My family lives in France, but my parents are gone. I have a house there, and I visit it each year. But it is different from when I was young."

"That sounds wonderful. I love it here because I love being near the ocean. My parents often vacationed on the North Carolina coast when I was growing up," Charlotte said.

"And what about your, Angie?" Michelle asked.

"You know, I came here for a different reason than what I am attached to now. I came here to fulfill a professional goal: to work as an architectural preservationist. Now, I almost feel like I have another purpose. Matt, my fiancé, wants me to consider where we should live after getting married. I didn't think that question would stump me so much. I assumed I would go wherever he was, but now that he has asked, I think I have some preferences. We were going to talk about that this weekend. He likes to plan for our future, while I tend not to plan for anything to avoid disappointment. Somehow, we will work on a decision that fits both of us."

"I hope to meet this gentleman sometime while he is here in town," Michelle said and continued. "Let me give you a tour of the house if you ladies would like. Our home is not as large as some here on the peninsula, but she has charm. The house next door is quite different on the inside. It has had more structural renovations with a distinctly modern style. Since Kyle liked the nautical presence and I liked the old European influences, our home feels more like you have walked back in time a bit. I like overstuffed chairs near windows so I can curl up and read. I also like rooms to have lots of light. Kye's area of the house is typical, with washes of grays and blues with a touch of color. He also likes heavier sculptures and darker artwork around him. I like soft and neutral fabrics, as I need them to calm my nerves; Kyle is very soothing when he is home."

"It's all lovely," Lauren said. She appreciated the artwork and textures the decorator used in furnishing the house.

Michelle graciously responded with, "Thank you. We love it too. It has a little mystery to it. Let me show you something we found in a hidden stairwell while remodeling the kitchen. Initially, the staircase went from behind a panel in the former butler's pantry next to the dining room, my husband believes. It later had a kitchen added on. We had to do some excavating and found the bones of an old stairwell that led to a tunnel below. It's all blocked in now, but at one time, it had gone to the wharf. We found a locket between the cracks that we believe had a hand-painted picture of the first lady of the house. There was some damage over the years, but we took it to a museum curator, who helped us find someone to restore it to a better condition than we found it. I keep it in the dining room. That was the tradition of the time to have the lady's portrait hung above the mantel. It's not that large of a piece, but we give her a place of honor on our mantel. Let's walk through this archway. I want to show you something in the other room. Michelle took the glass box that held the small miniature portrait hanging from a gold chain."

"It's lovely," Angie commented as she stared at the locket.

Charlotte added, "Angie, it looks like you."

"No, it doesn't." However, as Angie looked closer, she couldn't deny the resemblance.

"Perhaps it's just the hair color and blue eye," Michelle said, not to stir up conjecture.

"What do you think, Angie? Perhaps you would like to take a photo to compare it to something you have."

Angie looked at the portrait carefully. "Yes, I think Matt would love to do this. You say it was found in the stairwell of the dining room. Perhaps it had been dropped by the lady or man of the house as they were going out to the wharf through the tunnel. Interesting how something so small can say so much. She was beautiful."

"I would guess that it was completed for her engagement or wedding. See her necklace. That is what your dress needs, my dear. What you should wear with that dress is a piece of jewelry that speaks to you and is part of your portrait for your children and grandchildren to cherish."

"Yes, I like that idea very much," Angie said with a smile. "We have taken up so much of your time today, but I want you to know I enjoyed every moment. You have made this day so special for me!"

"Ah, that's what life is about," Michelle responded. She smiled warmly. "No, you let me take the dress to the shop and press and freshen it up. Then, when you give me a date, we will have it ready for you. Come to the shop and pay for it whenever you want. It will be there waiting."

"Thank you."

"Well, Angie, let's stop back at your place. We'll see if Matt is waiting. Maybe we can get him to lift that box of old bike parts Jarl gave him."

After thanking their hostess for a beautiful day, the trio returned to Angie's apartment. Matt was on the patio lounging out with the bunny, munching some grass on the patch of lawn, while Sam ran to the door to greet the incoming group.

"Hello there, friend," Angie said as she petted Sam's back. Matt made a turn of his head and waved from his perch.

"Well, it looked like you and your friends had a relaxing Saturday."

"I had to rough it today without you here, but now that you are, things look very promising."

"Hello, Lauren and Charlotte. Did you lovely ladies have an enjoyable day? Unfortunately, I didn't see the dress with you. Did you decide on one?"

"Yes, we did. It's fabulous!" Angie responded.

"We will let Angie tell you about the who experience, but it was a super day!" Lauren chimed in.

"Double wow for me!" Charlotte said, "Wow, for the dress and visiting Michelle Duvall at home. It was an incredible day, Angie. Thank you for inviting me. My days are never this exciting. I pick up a dress on a rack. Then I give the cashier my credit card. I've never had a fashion designer fit me for a dress and then serve me cakes and tea on the veranda. Pinch me, please. I'm sure I was dreaming after a night of too many pints of dark ale at the pub."

"Oh, that's too funny, but it was fun," Angie said. She was sifting through the cabinet to find the doggie biscuits she had stashed for Sam.

Matt figured out what she was looking for. He shook the box.

Angie laughed when she saw what he had and grabbed one for Sam. She kissed Matt on the cheek. "I loved it! Everything! I have so much to tell you, Matt."

Matt's unshaven jaw had a scratchy feeling today, but Angie decided it looked good on him.

"We are leaving, as it is obvious you want to be alone. But I have a box in the car, Matt. You can take off my hands if you want it." Lauren remarked.

"Oh, does that mean you have the part with you today?"

"Well, I have a lot of dirty-looking stuff in a box that Jarl said to hand over to you when I saw you. Unfortunately, I can't guarantee that it works or is what you need," Lauren said.

"You are an angel. Thanks! I'll get it and put it in my car." Matt said.

"The car is unlocked. You can't miss the box. Help yourself," Lauren responded and handed the fob over to Matt.

"I'll go right now," Matt replied. Then he went outside to check out what Lauren had brought.

"Come on, Charlotte, let us leave these two birds in love alone. We have a couple of turkeys at home to work on."

All 1 three young women giggled out the door. It had been a great day. They all had been nurtured by the hostess's kind invitation. It was a happy memory they shared.

"That was so fun! But I am ready to have some alone with you."

"The feeling is mutual," Matt said. "Sam Bugsy and I have had a pleasant visit. However, they aren't talkers. So, I had to pry it out of them where I might find the coffee beans. Bella gave me a clue with the twitch of her nose. Two twitches when I put a coffee mug beside her led me to cabinet number two. Thank goodness we speak the same language."

"You are so silly; I have some things to tell you and something to show you. Do you want to hear it now?

"Sure?" Matt replied.

"Okay. First, the dress is fabulous! It's exactly what I want and more. I can't wait for you to see it!" Angie was bursting with excitement. "The Duvall's home is incredible."

"I would expect no less," Matt said.

"Michelle, Mrs. Duvall showed us the house. Yes, it has been remodeled, but I would say many of the features of the original can be seen. The veranda at the back of the home is lovely. The rooms are decorated beautifully, but that's not what you would be interested in knowing. There was a tunnel from the house to the wharf. It was closed off but went from the old butler's pantry."

"There's the escape route," Matt said.

"They also found a small miniature lodged in the stone and brick of the stairwell. Since we found it, some work has been done to restore it, but it appears to be a miniature portrait of Kitty Van Dorn. I took a photo."

"You are kidding me! I want to see it!" Matt excitedly replied.

Angie grabbed her phone from her purse. It's right here. She opened the app and found the photo from earlier today. "This is it." Matt looked at the photo. "This is very interesting. I guess the Fitz men pick out blondes for their mates. She was stunning. Have you ever seen a portrait like this in your family heirlooms?"

"No, this is the only likeness I've ever seen of her. It is a painting, plus there has been some work to restore it so that some features may have been changed. However, it shows she was a beautiful lady and lived to be at least in her teens or early twenties, which we know. She looks young here. It would be interesting to know who did the restoration. The restorer was highly skilled in bringing the detail back."

"I know the referral came from the curator at the museum. I can find names of who they would suggest and follow up."

"You are becoming a real sleuth!"

"It's your influence, babe, just like sprinkling cinnamon in my coffee now because of you." Angie replied.

"I hope that spiciness generalizes." Matt teased.

"You are a mess."

"You've said that before," Matt replied.

"It hasn't changed." Angie teased.

"Nope, you can't change me. I am a hardcore mess inside and out. But you have made me softer and sunnier, which is good."

"Thank you for sharing that I am responsible for this irritatingly perfection of a mess I found."

Chapter 19

MATT RETURNED TO his home along the river. It was the middle of the week, and he was tinkering with a part on a workbench in his garage when he got a text to call Dr. Santoro when he was free.

Matt went to wash his hands at the faucet outside and dialed, putting the phone on speakerphone while he continued to work.

"Matt, I thought you might like some interesting information. We found some cannonballs near the shipwreck. Some cannon balls didn't match what would typically be used on an English boat frigate."

"Okay," Matt responded, still listening.

"We found cannon balls that look more like what would have been forged in the colonies and not what would have been on a sloop. One theory is that Captain Bodacious was the one that Hawke was after when the Constellation went down. The evidence doesn't quite match that story completely. Captain B was known for using a sloop, a much smaller boat that would not have that type of cannon. He was more likely to be moving people or small cargo that might need to go upriver. He was faster than the large merchant and naval ships. Hawke had been a commander of a large ship with armed men who had weapons. It wasn't a merchant ship that was defenseless. My thoughts are that Captain B's mission was never to attack a larger British vessel when he was in his sloop. That would have been suicide. There might have been tricky ways of downing a larger ship like Hawke's, like leading it towards a sand bar or through a narrow cove where the big ship would get stuck. But he would attack, especially in the open sea where that ship went down. He did not prey on other ships."

"I think there is another story about the shipwreck. I believe there was another ship on Hawke's wings. That's the ship that took down the. Constellation," said Dr. Santoro.

"Interesting," Matt replied.

His contact with Captain Hawke was reportedly when they made contact on land at different ports. Perhaps they crossed each other along the coastline. In that instance, Captain Bodacious would have had an advantage because of the speed of a sloop compared to a frigate and his ability to sneak into a cove or up a river where Hawke's vessel couldn't go. There was never a report where he attacked Captain Hawke in the open sea. I suspect that there was another vessel in the water that day. That ship was on the attack, and that was the one that brought the Constellation down. Perhaps the boat by sea was covering the back of Captain Bodacious. Maybe he was on a secret mission. The Constellation should not have been where it was. It doesn't make sense. Privateers and pirates were still around. Captain Hawke reported that Captain Bodacious was one of those rogues. But I have found no other reports or documents besides Hawke's influenced statements that imply that Captain B was like that. Captain Hawkes was not beloved by his crew or others who interacted with him. He must have been an intimidating figure. Nobody stood up to him, but nobody stood up for him. I am intrigued by the entire story."

"So am I. Matt said. I'm considering exploring the bluff like you mentioned when we were out diving. I asked Bob to go with me. We can get there by kayak. I will see what the state agencies will allow in exploring the area and if there's a road back there. A ranger can be with us, that's fine. It could be wild back in there. Bob said there's at least a pathway up the slope on the western shore of the barrier island that's almost directly opposite the site where the ship went down. I'll call you if I need you to pull some strings with a research permit."

"You bet. I'd have come with you if I wasn't diving at the site weekend. Maybe we can stop for a burger afterward on Saturday."

"You bet! Hey, do you know anything about German mountain bikes?"

"Afraid not, Matt," Bob said.

"Oh well, I will keep looking through this box a little longer. I'll talk to you soon. Good information!" *"Take care," Bob replied.*

The phone went silent. Matt stored the information in his mind. He was glad he had met up with someone that had a genuine interest in the story and was also a practical man with research skills. What had turned into a hobby had now become a passion.

Saturday had finally rolled around. Matt met Bob and stopped at the state's wildlife management office. Kayaks were permitted on the beach. That area was open to the public. However, the path up to the bluff was slightly more restrictive. Cutting, digging, or manipulating any part of the habitat was not permitted.

Matt and Bob got ready for paddling across the narrow water strip from the public access to the beach area of the barrier island. The water was smooth today and should not put up much resistance. If all went well, they'd be back by lunch before the sun started beating down. Mat had brought a simple waterproof camera to document the view and other interesting findings. Bob had a lot of historical diving experience and would have an essential insight into what may have happened to the Constellation. Storms and hurricanes had eroded the beach. Matt was sure the ocean had swallowed several feet of land over three hundred years. As they found their way to the path that went up the bluff, Matt noted some recent shoe marks. So, even though it was a restricted area, people had found their way there. After reaching the top, Matt observed the markings of a narrow path. There was evidence of a foundation for a building. Civil and revolutionary forts were built in the surrounding area. That would support the idea that civilization was on land near the wreck. Whatever builders were here were gone. It was difficult to say now if it was fire, wind, or neglect that pulled down the structure at this point. Perhaps an expert could find further clues about that. Matt would leave that for someone else to explore. They went closer to the edge. The view out to the ocean was spectacular on this cloudless day. Mat could see the boat where the divers were working in the distance. He could imagine that if there were survivors from the ship, it was possible and hopeful that row boats could have reached this bluff for safety. Were these the men that had witnessed the death of Captain Hawke? There were smaller harbors between here and Savannah along the coastal route. A couple of nautical miles up on another island, there was a lighthouse and a lighthouse keeper's dwelling. Those buildings had weathered the centuries and looked in good repair. Of course, that site was now owned and supported by the state government. Few people ever explored the area because of its remoteness and limited accessibility. However, it still was beautiful to look at by sea or as Matt and Bob were doing, from afar on another remote island. Matt knew the university had an archeological research site, so people occasionally visited the island. A lighthouse keeper still lived there and managed the maintenance of the buildings and grounds. Would an earlier structure have been present around the Revolutionary War? It's possible to put another item on Matt's research list. Communities occurred along the coastline, but even today, they were less dense than the areas along the industrial cities in the north. Back then, a British soldier could have easily slipped the lines and changed his loyalty, finding a hospitable hamlet to strangers. Matt heard a sound coming from below in the water. He turned around to look. He saw a motorized boat approaching the island from a deep cove across the watery passage. The ship had a familiar look. He has seen it in the area before, but the last time he saw it, or its twin was in Charleston. Bitters was gone, but the boats he piloted were still in operation. Matt was starting to get a bigger picture. When Matt was young, growing up in a small town up north, a local magistrate had gotten caught in a car theft ring. According to the town talk, he escaped to Mexico when the ring was busted.

Matt saw Bitters walking along the same line, but with different merchandise. "Bob, do you know what I see? I'm not sure that is a friendly boat. We got some cover, so I don't think it spots us. Our Kayaks are below on the other side. Let's see if we can get down to our kayaks. Hopefully, that boat will go further out from shore. Matt and his friend followed the path until the shrubbery cleared away, exposing the footpath. Matt could see the motorized boat coming around the heel of the island just offshore. I don't think we are going to make it to the kayaks.

"What makes you not trust that boat?" Bob questioned.

"I knew someone who used to pilot a boat like that. Bitters must have been doing it for extra cash. His shrimper was being repossessed. I tried to help him out with the bank to negotiate something. Now I think my client went dealing on the side, finding some backup income. The last time I saw him, he ran for a boat like this one. They left him when they knew the rescue chopper was covering him. They left him to die so they wouldn't be caught. That's my theory, anyway. Matt pulled out his phone. I can't get a signal out on my phone. Can you?"

"No, not right here. Bob said. If I could get out of this little gulley, I might."

"I don't want to take my chances of being seen yet. Some guys on the boat may know my face and think I've been looking for them if they are part of Bitter's old crew. But they are most likely not suspicious of you if they should see you. Ah Oh! Look who's coming over there."

Bob turned and saw what Matt was pointing out. "It looks like it's going to be a party on the island today as he saw another boat approaching from the opposite direction. Now, what do we do.?"

"Let us hold up for a moment and see if they meet. That boat, for sure, can see the kayaks on the beach." We can get closer to the beach, but we don't have any coverage once we are out of this maritime forest.

"I'm still watching what's happening out there in the water. It looks like our two boats have anchored."

Matt looked around, trying to find an escape. He then watched the larger boat take off and head directly east, away from the islands and land. He passed wide the research boat by a mile or so and kept going east.

Matt and Bob continued to move towards their kayaks under the canopy of trees and shrubs. They spotted their kayaks, but a shot was heard in their direction from the boat. "Run for cover. Go that way and see if you can get the Kayak. I'll run this way on the path and see if I can keep their attention on me. Stay covered until you think you can get away. Try to find a signal somewhere on your phone. I'll do the same. Be careful. I'm going to see what I can do from the east shore. Maybe I can get the attention of the research boat, and they'll call for some help. I may need to move higher on the bluff. Now go!"

Bob went farther west to where the Kayaks were left. Matt looked for a way to climb around the rocks and downed trees from a series of storms. The thick vegetation made each step arduous. There was not an easy way. The motorized boat was coming closer and around the island's front side, facing east. He wasn't sure if they were looking for him or had spotted someone or anyone. He wasn't sure what the shot was about. The boat continued slowly, coming closer to the shoreline, and then stopped, appear. He crawled to a cluster of blown-down tree trunks piled washed against a sandy dune. He grabbed some shrubs to pull as camouflage to make a visual barrier. What was he doing to do next? He could hear the boat start up and begin coming back around again. *Did Bob have his phone? Maybe he sent out a text.* Matt continued to hide. The motorboat went by again. This time, Matt saw the face of a man and had a sick pit in his stomach. *Bitters, you were right. Some evil men were there. The wolves were circling, and I fell right into their den. Matt heard a plane above.*

But he was afraid to flag it. Would Bob have a better opportunity? After a few minutes, the boat turned off its motor and waited. The predator was waiting for the prey to get out of his hole. Matt needed a miracle. And so he prayed.

Angie was getting somewhat worried after she had no messages from Matt by 2:00 PM. She called Matt's father, who also had concern in his voice. He knew what the plan had been; obviously, the project was now different. He, too, began making some calls. Matt should have seen or contacted someone by now, and there were no signs that had happened. Within the hour, people started spreading the word to find Matt and Bob.

From the ocean, Dr. Santoro spotted suspicious activity around the island from a distance. He had already called for his divers to return to the surface when he witnessed the partially sunken kayaks in the water. He updated the authorities with the new information and his knowledge of Matt's and Bob's day trip plans. Once the divers were back on board, Dr. Santoro headed for the island.

Matt was getting stiff, staying in one spot. *Somehow, he had to move without being seen. Fat chance of that happening.* He was running out of ideas.

The tide was also coming in, which meant he might need to go to higher ground. The boat just sat there waiting. Could something *come overhead that he could alert?* He was also feeling the effects of being dehydrated. He drank a couple of sips of water from his half-filled bottled water. *How much longer would he have to wait in this heat? He wasn't sure which.* Someone was coming off the boat and using a life raft to paddle to shore. Matt moved to run through the vegetation, knowing his body would not carry him far. He saw a spot over a small knoll that looked as if it had more cover. Matt felt a bullet graze his left shoulder. However, he continued to run for the mound, but tripped over something and fell into an old military entrenchment. Rocks had been pushed into the ditch, and as Matt fell, he felt acute pain as he struck something hard. He could neither see out nor move toward safer ground.

In the meantime, Bob continued attempts to signal the research vessel offshore. An escape plan was needed. There was an immediate danger, with the kayaks being deliberately untied and damaged, then released to the sea. Bob remained hidden behind a shed built by the rangers as a storage unit.

Matt had seen two armed men approaching the shore in a small, motorized craft resembling a small fishing boat. He was feeling trapped on an island with a few escapes on foot.

Bob was grateful to see the university logo on the ship's side as they approached the shore. He heard a gunshot in the distance and was weighing whether to run to the beach and attempt to swim to the boat or stay hidden. What was happening to Matt? If he could reach the craft, he could call for help from Matt. Was it already too late after hearing the shot? Bob listened carefully. He heard more sounds. Motorized sounds were coming closer. He heard boats' sounds and then heard something larger, powerful coming closer.

Coastal security personnel were arriving. Finally, Bob felt safe climbing out of the shed he had hidden and running to the help that had arrived.

A rescuer arrived on the beach within 10 minutes of Dr. Santoro's call. Drew Taylor's team came in an amphibious medical vehicle built to perform in water and land. Under the leadership of the CEO, the company was building a reputation as a premier provider of large machinery and safety equipment that could be on water and in wet environments. Taylor was on hand to watch the training demonstration for rescue operations with the latest line of equipment used for search and recovery for disaster situations. His company's trainers, rescuers, and medical crew were all present when the lighthouse keeper's office noted the emergency call to the authorities. The equipment was in the water in less than three minutes and ready with medical and rescue personnel that were already onsite. The officers alerted additional rescue teams, and support went to the island.

Matt drifted to a world of darkness. The next thing he knew, he heard a voice. Matt saw Naya and her hand reaching out to him. He shook his head and wrestled with the dream, as that was not the direction he wanted to go, with Naya pulling him through a cloud of fog. Matt then heard Angie's voice and pulled his hand out of Naya's. He felt the fear of leaving Angie and not seeing her again. Then he dreamed of himself swimming in clear water. He was trying to reach for Angie's hand while she was leaning from a boat. He heard her voice.

"Here I am. Reach my hand, Matt. Please reach it so I can pull you up. Don't let go of my hand. "Angie was wearing a white dress without sleeves and a necklace that looked like a pearl necklace with a heart-shaped locket that a young girl would wear. He had to touch her hand. He heard other voices and couldn't tell if they meant good or evil.

"Can you hear me? Matt, we're going to airlift you to a hospital. Don't move. When the chopper comes, we will slide you into the basket. Don't move, though. Try to stay as still as you can. That's the fastest way to get you to the hospital."

He heard Bob's voice near his ear. He tried to speak, but it hurt to catch his breath.

"You are okay. We think you may have broken some ribs when you fell, so we don't *want you to move. You can squeeze my hand if you hear me."*

Matt was pushing the fog out of his mind and tried to squeeze that hand that was holding his. His vision seemed blurred. He couldn't see the faces talking to him, yet he saw the faces in his dream. What was happening to him? There was a stabbing pain in the fleshy part of his shoulder, and he felt something wet on his shirt.

"Can you count how many fingers I have?" someone asked.

Matt shook his head. Matt whispered something in a quick burst. "Can't see anything."

Bob and those present heard but didn't let on their concern. Bob kept reassuring his friend. "Matt, we are almost out of here. I see the chopper now. We're going to get you out of here."

Matt recognized the voice. I'm not dreaming about this. He tried to move, but there were sharp areas of pain. He sent out another whisper. "Thank you," and then he went quiet.

The chopper came within the next five minutes, and the crew from the helicopter lowered the basket. The medical team, brought to the scene by Drew Taylor, were on the ground to assist. A flat board gently slid underneath Matt's body. He grimaced with pain. He allowed them to buckle him in with no resistance. Then Matt was raised off the ground and into the chopper. The door shut, and the mechanical bird took off.

The chopper's pilot made his announcement back to the command center. "Captain Bodacious on board, and the expected arrival time is 17 minutes to University Hospital. Requesting a surgeon for gunshot wound to the right upper arm, possible broken ribs on the left. The victim has lost vision. Over."

"Copy that. Awaiting arrival."

On the ground, Bob and Drew gave each other a high five. Then, the men walked from the earthen trench Matt had fallen into when he ran for higher ground and back to the beach. They could then recount the story away from the uninhabited island.

Dr. Santoro and his crew returned to the beach after taking a few minutes to examine the entrenchment. Dr. Santoro suspected the authorities would want to explore further the suspicious soil movement at this possible old fort site. There were signs of recent human behavior or abnormal ghost activity with shovels. Dr. Santoro was practical and had a theory that it wasn't the latter. The day's events supported Dr. Santoro's impression that Matt had mistakenly fallen into an operation of illegal workings that had been going on without detection.

Drew was amazed at what had happened and who was involved. The odds of him being so close by and onsite with his rescue equipment and the entire team were astronomical. The new equipment the company was introducing had some preorders, but nothing had been delivered to any of the company's customers yet. Drew had to admit his new amphibious land and sea rescuer got a rating of one hundred stars out of 10 today. As Drew assisted where he could and watched the professionals go into action, he felt he was following the path he was given in life. And if Matt recovered from his injuries, Drew felt sure he and Matt were partnering on the same road. Drew had played football long enough to learn a quarterback needs a strong running back. Drew believed he had just found the ace for the offense.

Two weeks later. Matt was being smothered with female attention as they propped him up on the bed with his pillows, a glass of iced tea, and a bowl of cereal. His mood instantly improved when the doctor allowed him to be discharged, if he had supervision and nursing care, and came in to monitor his mending for a few more weeks. The miracle was that his vision had returned within a couple of days because he may have hit the back of his head during the fall. The soft silty ground may have softened the blow to the head, but his ribs took the brunt of the fall on the rocks. His arm had just been grazed by a bullet that may have ricocheted off the rocks and would be as good as new. There were no signs of a bleed, and he was free of headaches.

"That feels better. It's scorching today. All I want is cereal right now. I'll ask for something else if I'm still hungry later."

"Do you think he's being pampered a little too much?" Angie asked teasingly.

"Oh, don't worry, dear. Matt's father was just as bad after he was in a vehicle accident in Germany. They pampered the wounded soldiers at her medical center more than a newborn, and Matt's father loved to make his nurses blush. I remember because I was one of those nurses. I was determined to pamper him until he was old, so I married him when asked. We are still together, and I still do the fussing and the fluffing over him."

Angie laughed and turned toward the patient. "Matt, do you want me to turn the TV on?"

"No, I'm good." Matt thought he needed a break from all the attention, especially from his parents. They hadn't left his side since he was admitted to the hospital and discharged. "Mom, why don't you and Dad go out and get something to eat because you both need a break? You've been stuck with me for several days. I have Angie here. I'll be fine."

Matt's dad got the hint. "That sounds like a good idea. I could use some fresh air, and so could your mother, Matt."

"Well, okay," Matt's mother said with hesitancy. Then, finally, she looked back at her husband and reluctantly gave in. "We won't go far and be away for too long. We'll let you two be along for a while."

"Thanks, Mom. Why don't you and Dad pick up some ice cream on the way back? I like vanilla ice cream with pecans and a swirl of chocolate. There's only one grocery store that carries it around here, the Shop and Bag, across the bridge. I might like some later tonight."

"Ah, it reminds me of when you came home from the hospital after getting your tonsils out. You asked for the same thing. All you wanted for a week was vanilla ice cream." Matt's mother held back her sniffles.

"Let's go before they buy all the ice cream, dear." Mr. Fitz understood the message completely. He knew the store was the farthest away, but that was still close enough to be reasonable. Matt was just like me when he was young and looked back at his son and winked.

Matt moved his lips to tell his dad, "Thank you," as his mother left the room to get a tissue and her purse.

Matt looked at Angie with a smile and waited to hear the front door close before he said any more. Then, when he heard his dad's car start, he looked at Angie. "I need some skin cream on my shoulders for my sunburn. You have the right touch."

"You were embarrassing me in front of your parents," Angie teased. "Don't worry about them. They are okay with leaving us alone. We haven't done anything they didn't do before they got married."

Angie took the tube and put some thick liquids in her hands. She started rubbing the substance on Matt's shoulders. "Let us know when you want visitors. Your friends have been reaching out and asking about you."

"Not yet. Maybe when my ribs aren't as tender. They hurt with every move right now. Can you move down to the shoulder blades a little?"

She moved her hands further down and then placed some more soothing ointment on her hands. She patted it gently on the reddened skin and glided it across the broad surface of Matt's back.

"I'm going to shed a lot after this. We can't get married until this old dead skin is gone. It will ruin the pictures."

Angie replied. "We can wait until you feel as good as new. As for the pictures, what will it matter if your back is shedding?"

"That's good. Right there is where it itches the most." Matt's muscles relaxed. He smiled with relief. Then, Matt opened his eyes and smiled while lifting his good arm to reach for Angie's jaw and grazed it with his hand. "I want to look my best." Matt grimaced again as he tried to move too far and laid his arm back with frustration.

"I know you are getting better, as you are being silly again. However, I am sorry that you hurt so much." Angie responded.

"I'm feeling quite fine just now. That feels so, so good on my back. I am frustrated that I can't be up and around as much as I want. I want to catch up on my work so much. Instead, God plopped me right here for a couple of weeks to slow me down and give me all the time to think."

"And what have you been thinking about?" Angie asked, wondering what would be on his mind with all that had happened.

"I am grateful to Drew Taylor and his team for finding me, along with Dr. Santoro and his crew's help. I can't forget my friend Bob. Then I heard that the monstrous amphibious contraption that he arrived in came over from the island with the lighthouse. What were the chances that all those folks would have been there and available? I am impressed. Only God could have put him at the right time and place on Saturday. I'm told the bad guys split when that thing came up around the island's tip. I know no one who at least some of the bad guys were and what they've been doing. Bitters knew what they were up to in the area. I'm sure of it. He kept me out of harm's way several times. Now that I know what was going on?"

"That says he didn't completely have a hard heart. It also makes me wonder if you take unnecessary risks?"

“I guess not on the first thing you said. On the second part, I don’t want to be that close to that kind of activity with smuggling and drugs, especially with us and our future. When you are a young buck, it’s different. It’s a thrill to take risks. Now I want to think about us.”

“Does that mean you have sowed your oats?” Angie teased.

“Oh, I don’t think so, not until I’m 80 something.? But my interests are different now. How about a little lower down my back, please? Oh, that’s good!”

Angie gave him a smirk. “I think baby lamb here is basking in all this fussing attention he’s getting. Do you think we are coddling him a bit too much?”

“Maybe just a pinch. But it feels so good. Don’t make me laugh or move, though. Then all the goodness disappears, and my ribs remind me why I need nurse Angie around, and I can’t be at the office working. Otherwise, I feel fine. I was about to say that Drew has offered me a role in the company. I was doing some smaller things for him, but he has offered to recommend me to the board as the lead legal consultant. You know I also have an MBA, so I have a business background. I could become interested in doing something else instead of law and contracts. There may be other opportunities to move around in other departments worldwide. I want to do something purposeful, like something positive in a different capacity. I think this might answer a prayer I had been making before this all happened.”

"Really? I love it, not that the injury brought you to a halt, but that you might find something in you that you didn't even know was there."

"Yes, me too. Drew and his family have robust ties with France, but there are also locations. I'm rather partial to you telling me about a hike you went on or a piece of poetry you read in Gaelic that you know so well. I hear you listening to your tapes in the morning," Matt said.

Angie blushed and responded, "Wow! That sounds exciting!

"Would you like to work for the company and maybe move away?" Matt asked.

"Well, yes, and yes. I've been thinking a lot about recent conversations my dad and I have had. I believe this opportunity may have come at a great time."

Angie was listening keenly. "I guess your mind has been busy while you've been home. Your mother and I thought you were sleeping with the pain medication."

"I have been reading my emails over the last few days when I'm awake. The meds make me forgetful and dizzy, but they don't kill the pain. I'd like to see if I could get away from taking the one tonight and see if I can sleep without it."

"Okay," Angie said as she continued to listen. She rubbed a little warm cloth over a scratch he had received over his left eye.

"If I accept the new offer, we could live closer to Charleston or Savannah. He has administration offices in either location. However, you want a larger city with more cultural opportunities and employment connections. I don't want you to grow old and bored with me. We could find something that is our dream house."
"I love it! Love all of it! I could give you a big hug!"

"Please, not now," Matt grimaced. "Keep that idea on hold for a couple of weeks. Afterward, you can kiss, hug, or massage me from head to toe for as long as you want. Ouch! My ribs need to mend a little more. Please don't make me talk anymore. I'm going to close my eyes now, okay?"

"Sleep, my precious one. I won't disturb you."

Angie sat back down in the wingback chair she had pulled beside the window in his home. She picked up a book she had been reading and continued where she had left off. When he woke up a couple of hours later, he asked for a bowl of cereal. When his dad brought it to his room, Matt was sleeping again, at least for another hour.

The following morning, Matt's mother was already caring for her son. Angie took a break, took a hot shower, washed her hair, and put on fresh clothes. She wandered into Matt's room a few hours after napping on the sofa. When she woke up, she poured herself some coffee and returned to Matt's room to check on the patient.

"Good morning," Matt said to Angie as she stood by the door.

"Good morning to you, too. How are you feeling?" Rough, but better. How about I give your mother and dad a break now that I'm up?

"I will vote for that," Matt said.

"Well, if you think it is okay. Your Dad and I can do some errands. We'll return and take you to your doctor's appointment at about 12:30."

"That should give us time." Matt looked over at Angie. He tried to sit up alone and waited to listen for the door to shut. "Now we're alone. Mom does well with the pillow fluffing, but you do much better with the back rubs. Could you get behind me and massage my back? Right on the blades would be good. Gently, please. Ahh, that feels so good. You know she makes me drink that herbal tea without caffeine or sugar. You at least bring me an iced tea or cola when I ask. I am incredibly grateful."

"You are spoiled!" Angie teased.

"I am, but you still love me anyway, right?"

"I'm thinking. Give me a minute."

"Let's get married, Angie," Matt said.

"We are someday soon."

Matt persisted with the request. "Let's get married on the first of October. That will give me time to get into the new job, and my body will completely heal. Then, you can take off the fall semester, or maybe there's a way to get credit for an independent study for the fall semester?"

"Yes, probably. You don't have to think about this stuff right now," Angie said.

"Yes, I do. I am the planner, remember? I let you be the spontaneous one."

"Okay then, let's plan for the first week in October. I don't like Halloween." Angie replied.

Matt smiled back. "I promise no ghosts or goblins invited."

Chapter 20

MATT'S ASSISTANT came to the office door, alerting him it was time to begin his journey. "Mr. Fitz, the limousine driver, is waiting out front."

"Thank you, Ms. Aniston. I guess I'm ready." He smiled at his assistant. Then, he walked out of the office and took the escalator down. Employees filled the lobby, sending Matt off with a banner that read, *Bon voyage*, Matt and Angie!

"Thank you," Matt said and waved goodbye before opening the door to push towards the parked car waiting for him.

"I have the bags that were sent down, sir. Is that all?"

Matt took a quick look and said, "Yes." Then he got in the back seat.

"I have your airline information already. Will we make any stops before the airport?" the driver asked.

Matt responded. "No, take me straight to check in, please." For ten weeks, Matt would be out of the country. He was taking this part of the journey alone and had much on his mind. However, the flight would give him some time to transition into his new life. He was thankful that he had made close to a full recovery. However, he didn't plan to volunteer for pickup soccer games for several months. Diving was not on his top list of activities, either. He was looking at his life through a different lens these days. Eleven hours of travel time gave him much time to reflect on this new adventure he was taking with Angie. There were things he didn't like about himself. *Would Angie notice and hate those things, too, eventually?* He tossed those thoughts away, knowing they were part of the bars of insecurity that held him in darkness after Naya's passing. He had grown to be a different man now.

Less than Forty-eight hours after leaving Charleston, Matt stood outside an old stone chapel in a small village in northeastern France. Jarl had gone inside to make sure everything was in place. He returned soon after to tell Matt everything was in order. Matt eagerly awaited the cars to appear around the bend in the lane that brought Angie and her parents to the chapel.

Angie had asked for a simple wedding with the immediate family. But, of course, she wanted her friend Laurel to fix her hair. A small chapel in the foothills of the Alps staying at a guest house on a nearby 26-acre estate was the chosen setting. It was an opportunity from the Duvalls, who owned the property as part of Mrs. Duvall's inheritance. The older couple had become friends with Matt and Angie over the past few months, as they had a lot in common and felt this would make a lovely wedding present. The only guests were the parents of the bride and groom. Plus, Jarl and Lauren, who served as hairdressers, makeup artists, photographers, shuttle drivers, and couriers. As for Michelle Duvall, she invited herself. For the bridal shop owner, bringing the dress from the states and sharing her parent's former home and gardens with the wedding entourage was a delight.

It was a beautiful, clear fall day, just as Angie had initially talked about wanting for her wedding in her hometown in New York near. Matt hoped this compromise would be a winning alternative for both. Thinking no ghosts would take away from what should be the happiest day of their lives, the chapel seemed ideal. Little did he know what rode the wind down from the mountain tops and under the doors and crevices of the old stone structure. The vehicles finally made their way around the bend, past the stacked stones lining the lane, and to the front of the church, where they stopped to let people out.

Matt greeted his parents, who were in the first car to appear, and Lauren and Angie's mother, who followed along in the second car just a few minutes later. He waited for Angie, but she wasn't part of the first two cars. His face showed confusion and disappointment. Finally, however, the elder, Mr. Fitz, took his son by the arm and led him to the entrance door of the church.

"Wait here, son," he said. A few moments later, another car drove up and stopped. Angie's father stepped out, opening the car door and allowing the most exquisite woman Mat had ever seen to walk slowly towards him. She wore a long white cape. The cape had a hood, which she wore up as she left the car. Jarl held the door open for Matt and his father while they proceeded to the front of the chapel. With Matt waiting at the front and his father meeting up again with his wife, Matt stood alone to watch Angie be escorted by her father to the front of the church.

Once Angie made it inside the chapel. She unbuttoned the sole pearl clasp that held the cape together at the neckline and took the wrap off to give to Lauren. Angie's hair was styled to allow spiraling curls to fall, the right shoulder cascading past her collarbone. Her complexion was like milk, and her lipstick was vibrant with a violet, red hue. The other colors of her face were faint except for her sparking blue eyes that jumped out from beneath her black lashes. She wore a pearl and diamond pendant suspended on a silver chain that had been a gift from her mother. It had been a piece of jewelry passed down from the Van Dorn family and had been in safekeeping until Angie was old enough to appreciate the family heirloom.

Matt saw a vixen of innocence and vitality. *Was this the same woman who was seen wearing a T-shirt and shorts and running on the harbor's edge? Sweat pouring down her back and into her brows on a humid Carolina day? Yet here she was, standing by his side in a centuries-old chapel across the waters.*

Angie had asked for pink roses for her wedding. Therefore, Matt arranged for a bouquet of thornless stemmed roses tied with white satin to arrive at the guest house this morning. She had the bouquet but reached for something in a silk bag. She unwrapped a single rose with a diamond lapel pin and placed it above his coat pocket like a boutonniere.

"Now you are quite perfect, Mr. Fitz."

"You've stolen my sweet Angie and brought me an angel. He whispered in her ear."

Though the bride and groom were connected in the present, there were those present who were not surprised to feel the whispers and touch of the wind. It swept in swirls of sparking snowflakes carried down from the peaks, sparkling like glitter and landing on the panes and stone before melting away. The stone and mortar could not hold back the celebration of love, just as it had welcomed the captain and his bride three hundred years earlier.

The couple said their vows in French and English. Matt's mother also read three scripture verses in English. Angie's mother read the verses in French as she spoke the language fluently. After the ceremony, a light luncheon was waiting back at the estate. There, a lovely view of the mountain tops covered with snow contrasted with the colored fall foliage fluttering in the surrounding breeze. The atmosphere was simple and rustic, encircled by those Matt and Angie loved.

Soon, the couple would return to the ordinary things of life, like taking Sam for a walk and cleaning the leaves from the gutter. However, at this moment, the fairytale existed, and the crazy demands of life ceased. The air whistling through the canyons flowed towards making peace with the sea several hundreds of miles away. There it would become one with salty air and float across the ocean to the salty beginnings on another shore.

Chapter 21

ANGIE WAS EAGER to put things in their places since they moved into their new home. "Matt, where do you want me to put all this stuff? Your dad brought it over today before he and your mom checked into their rental on the beach. I don't want to put it in the garage."

"Here, I will take it and put it in the closet in the room that will be my office. Then I'll unpack it later." Matt said.

"Thanks. It helped me clear a space for the entry table."

"You did a lot of work without me today. I'm impressed. You did a lot of work. I'm sorry I wasn't more help."

"Lauren and I did better without you being around. That way, you couldn't argue with our ideas. She left just a little while ago," Angie responded.

"Well, I guess that tells me I'm not always wanted around to get in your hair."

"That's not true. I love it when you're around, but not when I'm working. You distract me too much!"

"Like right now. I feel we should take a break. I am tired, and I bet you are too. Could I talk you into ordering dinner at McCabe's up the street? I'll pick it up."

"Sure. I'll call in an order," Angie said.

Matt was on his way twenty minutes later, so Angie took a quick shower and cleared a space for dinner. She was happy to freshen up after the physical labor in the heat of the Carolina summer.

When he returned, Matt smelled the fragrance of bath oil. Then, being the gentleman, he let his presence known by calling out, "I'm back." However, he thought, *I may not want dinner after all.*

Matt went to the kitchen and laid everything out on the counter. He began food preparation by grabbing a lemon, squeezing the citrus into the cup, and pouring oil. Before he could put the bottle down, he stopped what he was doing.

"I found this today while snooping around in some of my things. I had forgotten about this after you were hurt. It wasn't even on my mind, and then the wedding plans drastically changed because I..."

Matt raised his finger to his lips to stop Angie from saying anything. Instead, he walked over to her with his eyes sparking and the corners of his cheeks lifting, showing his deep smile lines. "It was probably safe to keep this hidden while I was still hurting, but to keep it hidden now would be wrong."

"I didn't want you to think me presumptuous," Angie whispered with a smile.

"Oh, presumptuous is very much what I like about you. May I say that this is a perfect evening for you to be presumptuous? So, this is the 'bomb' you've been warning me about all those weeks before I went on that island to explore. I wouldn't have gone to the darn island. If I had known you had that in your arsenal that weekend, I can assure you of that. I would have surrendered to your charms and given up my ways of dangerous dives. Without resisting, I would have handed over my boat's keys and treasure in the cooler. Captain Bodacious would have fled from his life of danger, stayed here, and safely guarded this. Matt came closer and kissed her."

"You would have done that for me?"

"I spent my lifetime looking for you at every sunset and every wave that reached me. I would gladly give everything else away when I found a unique treasure. You are my pearls and diamonds, worth more than would ever fill a pirate's chest."

"You are good with words, Mr. Fitz. Did they teach you that in law school?"

"Oh no. Those words came from right here, and Matt reached for a hand to press it on his heart."

Chapter 22

SIX MONTHS LATER, Matt was getting the leash with Sam at attention at the door. It was a beautiful Saturday morning, and Matt would take his trusty companion down to the marina and back. When he walked out onto the porch, he saw a where a courier had delivered a box from Dr. Santoro. Matt was eager to open that, but it could wait until his return for the walk. Sam was excited to make the neighborhood rounds. Matt took a different direction this morning and headed for the small beach area within walking distance. The tide was low, and the sound was compacted, making walking easier this morning. A few shells and jellyfish were abandoned on the beach, dog and owner kept walking. Matt had so many things to share with God this morning. Gratitude for life was his first subject. Humility in each moment came next. Prayers for those he knew needed them in his sphere of friends were made as the tide rolled in and away. He left forgiveness till the end, as he figured that would be the most challenging part of his morning ritual. After the morning walk of solitude, Matt was ready to return.

Angie had put the package he had seen earlier on his desk. Sam, the friend to all, deserted him once man and dog had returned. Sam, preferring the aroma from the kitchen, scampered off in that direction.

Matt, curious to open the package, went straight to his desk. He opened it and found a manuscript inside. The contents, including a chapter on Captain Bodacious, Matt turned to the first chapter.

Was he real, or was he a myth? Unfortunately, the story around Captain Bodacious may never be known. His name is fictional, and his presence in the 1700s on the eastern shore is murky. However, legend says he was deeply loved, and rumors spread that the continental militia's highest power protected him. Documents reveal pure hated by at least one English Captain. This chapter provides some facts about what we know.

Matt closed the book and laughed. I think I know how it ends. A piece of paper fell out of the back of the book. Matt opened it up.

There was a picture of a tiny cross made of pearls and diamond studs. The note read.

I can't send you the genuine necklace, but sketches of it can be seen at the museum at Captain Hill's farm. He was a shipbuilder, specifically sloops and schooners. He married Kitty Van Dorn Hawke from Charleston soon after Captain Hawke's ship, the Constellation of the British Royal Navy, went off the Georgia coast around Sept. 1777. They sold the house shortly after the war ended and went to New York. Captain Hill had a friend, Luke Shaw, also a shipbuilder in the Philadelphia area. He came over as an indentured servant on the same ship as the Van Dorn family, who became well known for shipbuilding in the same area. Shaw had a bounty on his head because of Captain Hawke. He may have been jealous of friendships between Van Dorn and Shaw, who worked and was promoted by Kitty's father in the business. It seems like there was some shadiness about Hawke, who extorted from Dorn and was forced to marry his daughter to Captain Hawke.

I don't get into all the romance links in the story, but there are some mysterious bends. It seems like Luke was linked to being Capt. Bodacious by Captain Hawke is never written or spoken about after September 1977. Captain Hill saves the day and takes down a British frigate off the coast of Georgia in September 1777. The shipwreck we were researching appears to be Hawke's frigate, and that ship was not brought down by a sloop from what we can see.

Evidence shows that Captain Hill's ship was further out in the ocean, shooting toward the frigate. I just thought you would like to know. There was some outlandish rumor that a French General was on board with some supplies for the colonies on the Hill's ship. Maybe that wasn't a rumor, as the French provided ships and military support during the Revolutionary War. Hawke went down because he was chasing the sloop for a personal vendetta was my take. Hills' ship met him at the pass. That is how I would interpret what happened. The sailors saved from the sinking ship were reportedly treated well by the Captain Hill. As a result, many swore allegiance to the side of the colonies when the boat anchored near a fort outside of Savannah. Others found their way back to England. That might be why nobody questioned who the actual Captain Hill was that day. The real Captain Hill had no family and no ties. There's some evidence that he may have been ill and given the command of his ship to a known officer, Captain Luke Shaw, to run the command. He may have been protecting the Sloop. Likely, he knew who was on the sloop. Maybe the sloop was going to trade cargos, so to speak. I suspect the men on Hill's vessel were loyal to Captain Bodacious, given his reputation and the precious cargo they were hauling. Maybe Captain Bodacious wore many hats. He appears to be this mythic shadow like person. Stranger things have happened. I just thought you should know. The necklace in this picture resembles what you were babbling about when we found you. It was Kitty Van Dorn's from when she was a small child given to her by her father. It was one of the few things she brought to the new world but lost on the boat. Maybe somebody took it or had kept it for safekeeping.

Best wishes,

Ben Santoro

Angie's footsteps could now be heard in the hallway. Matt folded the letter and got up to meet his wife, who was carrying a mug of coffee.

"I thought I'd bring you some while it's still fresh."

"Yes, thanks." He kissed her.

"Anything interesting in the box?" Angie asked.

"Yes, sort of. Ben sent me his manuscript that he's been working on regarding Shipwrecks off the eastern coast. It's a research thing. He must produce a certain amount of published work as a professor to keep his grants. Some of it's interesting. I'll read it when I get time. Maybe I'll give it to Dad, has might enjoy reading it. Keeping my wife happy and finding my new leg at work is about all I have time for now."

"I am very easy to please." Angie teased and came around the chair to message his shoulders. "However, I would like to start in the spare bedroom today. Let's finish first, as I want it ready when our family comes to visit."

"Sure," Matt laughed. "Let me know what I can do to help you." Matt knew this would be another day, with the morning devoted to the house. He had to accept that there were many things like this in marriage. Matt's mind was filled with some things he had heard the guys say about marriage, but Matt didn't believe that was true or fair. He loved being with Angie, even if it was hanging pictures up down the hallway or sweeping the living room while she washed the dishes before company came. She made the routine things in life fun. Matt would defend her on that point with any of his guy friends .*When she goes to flee the market in a pair of jean t shorts and one of his T-shirts, she is a vision. And when she spins around on the stool while she's painting a wall in the pantry, listening to the lyrics to some old rock classics, I can't think of anything more entertaining. She wasn't even on the planet when those songs were big. But, when she does laundry to rhythm and blues, it's taken to a new level.* Matt laughed. *What did Angie think about me since we got married?* He looked over at her while choosing which curtain she wanted to hang. He was hoping she couldn't read his thoughts.

Angie was thrilled when Cassie mentioned a house going up for sale in her lane. It was a few houses away from Cassie and Bradley's homes. It was smaller than others on the street, but it was lovely inside. Angie and Matt were happy to have instant friendships as neighbors close by after the wedding to help them adjust to their new life together. The first thing Matt had requested was a sleeper swing on the back screened-in porch. She had a handyperson put it up while Matt was on a business trip to the west coast. When he entered the door, Angie asked for his laptop, phone, and tie. She took him back to the porch and showed him the new piece of furniture. Dinner was out on the patio that night as Matt tried out his new favorite hangout.

The decorating Matt left for Angie. He cooperated with speaking up about what he wanted. Angie chose artwork, particularly in the dining room and living room, where most friends and family gathered. She found a gallery on the peninsula and found the perfect watercolor pieces. However, Matt made it known that a copy of the portrait from a photo taken in France went into his office. Angie used her painting skills to make a likeness of the women in the locket found in the Duvall home. It was placed underneath the captain in a frame on the bookshelf. Angie's version had her sitting on the sloop's bow, her hair blowing in the breeze, looking towards the shore. She put an engraved message on the plaque.

Salty beginnings are where tide and sand collide, and love lasts forever in the wake.

Since her return from the honeymoon, Angie had questions. What was she expecting out of marriage? What was Matt expecting of her? She thought about that after a phone conversation with Lauren, who had yet to marry her long-time partner, Jarl.

Angie wasn't sure where she was with her dream of being happy forever with Matt. She had been independent before getting married. It was odd thinking of someone else in the decision-making process. She felt the need to lean on her faith now because living daily on her wisdom wasn't good enough when someone else was in the picture. She still needed her independent time. Matt was great about letting her work and doing what she wanted. However, she also knew that some choices wouldn't be good for her relationship with Matt if she made them. Angie arranged her work so that it allowed for free weekends and evenings with Matt when he was home. Maybe she was brought up old-fashioned, but she loved how her parents had kept their relationship fresh all these years, yet they both had very active lives. They kept the intimacy and caring strong between them. The Duvalls appeared to have that same chemistry. They enjoyed being with one another as people. I think they both like being who they are individually and together. That's a lot of work, Angie thought. She knew it would be, but the reality of an ongoing project was scary to Angie. I want it to work; I don't want things to fail, and the more I fill myself with *fear and insecurity, the more things don't go right.* There were too many questions for Angie to face. She was only in the first year of this agreement to marry this guy who likes to work on mountain bikes, scuba dives, and reads volumes of books. But, she wondered, *does Matt have the same anxieties about how to make things work as she did?*

Angie posed the question to Matt one night after dinner while walking on the beach near their home.

"I've had this song rolling through my head all day today." "And what is that?" Matt asked.

"Don't ask me the name. It's an old one from before I was born. It would have been something my parents would have played." "I get it. What decade?" Matt questioned.

"I don't know, 1970 to 1980 probably," Angie replied.

"Okay, there was some good stuff in those years." Matt teased. "Go on and tell me what's on your mind."

"I'm just going to put this simply. I don't know how to keep our relationship strong and not go down the ski slope into the ski line with a crash, as many of my acquaintances have done." Angie replied.

"Well, I know the sentiment. I've never quite heard it spoken in such a creative way." Matt paused before answering to think through his answer. "Does it make you feel better that I have the same fears?"

"Not really, unless you have the answer."

"I don't have the answer," Matt said. "How will our lives be in 20 years? I suspect that's our job to figure it out. We've taken this road and are committed to it. What does it look like when my income isn't what it is now? I don't know. Will you be happy with me if I can only pick a rose from the neighbor's garden instead of taking you to Italy for our anniversary?"

"Did you say Italy?" Angie looked at him with keen eyes.

Matt nodded his head affirmatively. "Perhaps you would prefer Ireland and Scotland instead?"

Angie's eyes lit up with excitement. However, she didn't miss the true meaning behind the question. "Wait a minute, that's a trick question. But, of course, I would love you the same. You didn't change because you gave me a rose instead of some fancy trip. I am happy when I can sit in the same room when you are reading a book."

"Thank you. What about if I became disabled like someone who has had a stroke? I can't tell you I love every morning while your head is still on the pillow. Will you still love me then?" Matt asked in earnestness.

"I would love you more because you needed more love." Angie put her arms around his neck and looked straight into his eyes. "Let me flip the story. What will happen when I find I can't wear a size four anymore, an eight, or even a ten? Will your love grow less because I grew more around the waist?"

"I'm going, to be honest. I love you when you're like this—a beautiful woman. My memory will always remember you like this. That's true even when you are in your nineties. If I'm breathing, I still will see the lovely young lady who sat across the table with me on the very first day I met you. The sun glistened on our highlights and cheeks. The white blouse was buttoned just a tad below your collarbone. You wore an aquamarine stone on a silver chain around your neck that peaked through when you moved. The lipstick was bright poppy pink. I prefer that hue over neutral pink, especially on a sunny day. I remember all of that."

"Okay, with all the details. You took in a lot more information than I thought. That was *a pretty terrific answer," Angie responded.* She looked up at him with tears rimming her eyes.

"I can't argue with you about that, and I won't stand in your way of becoming that person. But honestly, I don't know what that person looks like for you or me. I'm not sure if this provides any answers to your questions. I suspect I will figure it out as we go, just like our parents did. Do you think my dad knew how to change my diaper as a baby? Not a chance. He learned after times of failing, multiple times, I'm sure."

As they returned home, Matt stopped when they reached the front porch. By now, the sun had nearly set, and the stars were showing themselves in the sky.

"So, I was being silly this evening?" Angie said.

"No, you were not being silly at all. You were asking the most important questions of all. You are just asking them of a person who does not have the answers. Matt pointed at the star that was making itself present in the northern sky. Whenever we are apart, I'm looking for that star at night. I know that wherever you are, you can see it too, and it's looking down on us. It knows who has the wisdom and light to unite and protect us."

"I just thought of something. My mother gave me my grandmother's pendant to wear at our wedding. She said the pearls represented wisdom, and the diamonds represented life. My friend Michelle told me to wear a necklace that would mean something special at my wedding. I guess I did. The pendant will mean a lot more to me now. Was there something sentimental you had in a pocket or a shoe at our wedding?"

"I wore my fancy bow tie at the ceremony, which matched my black lucky socks? Does that count?" Matt teased.

"No," Angie said.

"I'm looking for something, Angie. It was something I remember when I was coming out of consciousness on the island. I think it's still out somewhere, wanting to be found or at least seen again. It has a meaning like a pendant to you. I want to see it and know it existed, not just in my imagination."

"That sounds significant. Do you want to tell me what it is?" Angie asked.

"Not know. Maybe someday," Matt replied.

Angie stored that thought in her mind and let Matt find his way to the shower first. She had a few more things to put away and pondered everything she and Matt had discussed that evening.

The following morning, Matt prepared for work. He had poured himself a small glass of juice and gulped that down. Then grabbed a coffee mug and poured himself a cup while he took it outside on the screened-in porch to feel the m morning air and prepare his mind for work. He was used to Angie not bothering him during his early morning private time. So, when he came back indoors to put the cup in the sink, she surprised him by being fully dressed in a pretty silk dress and skirt.

"Last night, I didn't want to spoil our conversation. This morning, I have a meeting," Angie said. "I am talking with someone group of people and think I'm going somewhere different in my career. I'll tell you about it when you come home tonight."

"Okay, I love your surprises. Are you not going to tell me anything now?" Matt asked.

"No," Angie smiled. She kissed him on the cheek and went to the door.

"Come, we'll both be late if we don't get on the highway."

"Woman, I think you will keep me chasing after you all my days?" Matt teased.

"Like a deer in the forest," Angie replied.

"Lord, help me, but I do not want to go to work today. But I will, so you can tell me all about it. Okay. I'll be eagerly waiting to hear of your plans."

"Thank you, let's go," Angie said, and they both headed out for their cars.

Three hours later, Matt texted Angie, asking for a hint.

Angie responded. Spinach and sailors.

Matt was stumped. He texted during his next break. "Does it have to do with animation?"

Angie texted right back. *No, and no more hints!*

Matt looked over at the project manager. "I think I'm way over my head on this one."

"That's not true. You're the best man for this role," the man across the table said.

"Not on this," Matt smiled. "On being married. I was never so confused and confounded after meeting my wife."

"Oh yeah, it's part of the package."

Later that night, over dinner at home, Angie was ready to share the day's events with Matt.

"So that's what you have been hiding from me all day," Matt said. He sat down with Angie on the swing. "So, what did you say?"

"I told the Admiral and Dr. Gibbs I was thrilled by the honor. And yes, I would love to work on this project with them. I think it's a fabulous idea to have a state-of-the-art facility geared to wellness for active duty and veterans in the low county. It could be a pro-type for the center's regional centers throughout the United States.

There are already veteran hospitals and outpatient clinics in some communities. I love keeping the mind, body, and spirit healthy for service members and women, especially in areas heavily affected by the military. I remember growing up where there was a rehabilitation facility. That was the place to go if you were injured. It was not antiseptic at all. It was a fabulous place to work and recover. That's what I'm thinking, but in this setting, as it is unique to this region for the purpose for which it was designed."

"I think it is a great opportunity."

"When you came back after Naya's death. You needed some place to heal. So, I want to build a place to honor her life. She was special to you, and her spirit deserves that honor. When she loved you, she gave you a gift. You gave me the gift when you shared your love with me.

"Now I want to share that gift with others."

"Wow, I'm touched, Angie."

"I don't know what to say. However, I think it's wonderful to use one's talents to better the lives of others. I am a fortunate man to have you as my wife."

"I won't argue with the last part. We are better than partners. We are greater together than apart."

"Yes" But I am afraid what will happen when my warts start showing."

"You'll still be you. I think I would miss the warts most of all because that keeps you human.."

Chapter 23

NEW YORK WITH enthusiasm. Angie went through online shopping sites for men's and women's clothing that were popular in colder areas, like Colorado and Maine. Matt would be miserable in his current wardrobe. His dress overcoat would work for church services. However, not for the lively antics of her family when they went looking for the right Christmas tree. Matt knew the cold fall temperatures and transitioning weather from fall to winter from being at the academy. But Angie wanted Matt to feel the vitality of when he lived there before, fearless and untamed. She had put too much energy into nursing him back to health, only to let him get sick while visiting her parents.

Matt was happy to spend a few nights at Angie's parents' home, as he liked the Van Dorns, but he also reserved some time for himself and Angie away from the family. It paid off, as the week was a hectic whirl of dashing, visiting, talking, and entertaining. Cold as it may be, with the nakedness of the trees after the fall foliage season had come and gone, there were still things to see and do. Matt had wanted to drive down to Pennsylvania. He wanted to investigate something his friend, Dr. Santoro, had discovered while researching shipwrecks. When Matt told Angie about the side trip he would like to make, Angie agreed.

"This kind of reminds me of our honeymoon," Angie said as they found a place to parallel park along a side street in a small village that meandered along a creek. They got out of the car and strolled toward the center of town. A vibrant art community had heavily influenced the town. Many of the shops were filled with galleries and locally crafted works. There was evidence of skills almost lost to history, yet it gave the town an old European flavor with a young soul.

"It reminds me of the little towns in northern France."

"What did you want to see here, Matt?"

"I don't know. Maybe nothing. Maybe this was one of those trails that doesn't go anywhere? Dr. Santoro had mentioned something to me once. I had done some reading on my own as well." Matt replied. "I just wanted to see if any clues were left after all these years." They walked down four blocks from the village square in the north and south directions. Matt saw nothing like he thought he might find in either direction.

"Let's run inside there and get some coffee before we head out," Matt said, trying to hide his disappointment. "I'm not used to the cold anymore, which makes my ribs ache a little."

Angie was happy to comply. They strolled into a coffee shop and sat down to warm themselves. A cozy fireplace burned with gas logs, a modern convenience, but it heated the room and provided atmosphere.

"What are you thinking, Matt?" Angie asked.

"I don't know. I liked the law because I enjoyed researching the details and developing a story. Finding the truth motivated me. Now I'd like to see life from a different angle."

Angie smiled back and shook her head. "Yes."

They walked outside into the cool air. Snowflakes fell from the gray clouds overhead as they returned to the car.

"We are not in Charleston anymore, are we?" Matt teased.

"It's still beautiful, though. I like snow around Thanksgiving and Christmas. It's like adding nature's decorations to the scene."

"I like snow too when I have a nice brandy and a pretty blonde to hug," Matt replied.

"I think I can put that on your Christmas list as long as you've been a good boy this year."

"Oh yeah! I've been excellent this year," Matt teased. He opened the door for Angie, and they returned to their vehicle.

Something caught Matt's eye as they drove towards the main highway again. "There it is." Matt immediately took a left turn across traffic and turned into a small lane. The sign read. Nautical Museum and Lackawanna Recreational Center.

"Do you think the museum is open?" Angie asked. There were a couple of cars in the parking lot, but that may be for those brave enough to walk along the river in this cold.

Matt turned the nob, and it turned. He ushered Angie inside and made a quick look around inside.

"Well, come on in," Matt heard a man said, as he saw a man approaching them from another room. "Get yourself out of the cold!"

"Thank you. We weren't sure you were open."

"It's the holidays and the weather keeping people away today. However, the walking trails around the old farm are very popular."

"So, this was the farm?" Matt asked.

"Yes, the property was Captain Hill's farm after the revolutionary war. He had about six hundred acres in the original homestead. It changed hands a few times, and eventually, the grounds were donated to the state. I have a little pamphlet here about the history of the captain and the county. Let me see. Here it is."

Matt looked. "There's no picture of the captain?"

"No, the historical foundation never found a portrait of the captain. However, there have been rumors that a portrait hung in the original homestead when he and his wife lived there. Perhaps it went to one of the family members over the years." "Indeed. Perhaps." Matt responded.

"There are known portraits of his wife, Kitty. She was quite a lovely woman in her time. Perhaps the battle-handed captain didn't think his face would shine well against his wife's."

Matt showed Angie the photo on the brochure of Kitty Van Dorn Hill.

"It looks like the one in the locket," Angie responded.

"Do you have many things from when the captain and his wife lived here?"

"A few things. Captain Hill was a shipbuilder by trade early on, so we have some of his tools and drawings. One of his sloops is in the barn that you can look at. We keep it here to protect it. We have some of his writings before the end of the war. Ship logs and purchase receipts, but not a lot afterward. The family appears to have taken most of the personal items. Captain Thompson reportedly handpicked what he wanted to save. He burned most of his correspondence. There are some handmade pieces of furniture that the captain made himself, and a chest was saved. There were the items that were gifted to the family. Other things have been donated over the years. Please look inside at the displays. Please let me know if I can provide any further help in answering your questions."

Angie smiled brightly and replied. "Thank you so much. I am a Van Dorn from New York. My husband and I live in Charleston now. It's been interesting listening to the family stories."

"Oh yes. I hope you enjoy your trip. We have some donated things that were part of when the Hills owned the property. The other owners of the home have also added to the collection. You will find some of the larger tools used for shipbuilding at the barn. Once they moved here, Captain Hill spent his time on other things, like having a sawmill. He also worked with construction and invested in the railroad. That was probably in his older years; by then, he had moved on to another location."

"Can you tell us a little more about the adopted son?"

"That would have been Colin Fitz. He inherited the homestead and sold the property after Captain Hill passed on. From what I understand, he continued to make his fortune in coal mining and railroads. He ended up moving away. There were two daughters that Captain Hill and Kitty Van Dorn had. The eldest daughter died young and is buried next to her parents on the property in a grove of trees on a bluff at the river's bend. The youngest of their daughters married a second cousin named Miles Van Dorn. I bet you are from that line of the family. The Van Dorns were shipbuilders, too. They lived closer to the big city, where all the family business was. I bet you could find more information about them from the historical organizations representing areas closer to the city. I don't want to bore you now, so check out our displays if you can tolerate the cold. The property has a lot of interesting things to see as well. The best time to come is in the summer when we open the creamery. It's the best ice cream around. You know, I remember something you will have a special interest in. Being from Charleston and having the Van Dorn, you'll want to see this."

"I would like to see that very much," Matt responded. He reached for Angie's hand and followed the man to the next room.

"Here we go. This sketch was done of Miss. Van Dorn on a boat as a young girl. It's a rough sketch. It looks like someone on board had drawn her face looking out into the sea. There's another one when she's a young woman sitting in a garden. Palms and camellias are behind her. I assume it was from when she lived in Charleston. They are right here on the captain's desk. The story is that Captain Hill specifically wished to keep the three items together according to his will. Either they meant a lot to him, or they told a story that he wanted told about his life after he was gone?"

"Thank you so much for your information," Matt told the man. "We are going to enjoy walking through the museum. I'm sure my wife will enjoy this as much as I will." Matt waited until the host went to the other room before further investigating the images. Matt's eye stared at the necklace drawn around the child's neck. "That's the one," Matt whispered. He showed Angie. "Have you seen that necklace before?"

Angie shook her head. "No. I'm sure it was popular for young girls her age to wear that. It was probably a gift from a parent or grandparents."

Matt looked at it for several minutes. "I think he sketched her on the boat coming over."

"Who?" Angie asked.

"Captain B, but he was not a captain, then. He was an indentured first mate on the boat she traveled to America."

"What are you saying.?" Angie asked.

"They met on that ship crossing the Atlantic. She was a mere girl, and he was a slightly older boy, only a few years apart, but worlds apart in social status. That's their beginning, Angie! There was a connection from that time forward. I'm not a dreamer. I need to know the evidence before I believe it. But I love lining up the clues! The beginning is right in front of us. He left a message for anyone who cared enough to know the true story."

"The second picture looks like it was sketched in the backyard of the Duvall's home. That's where she lived. I don't know if this would have been when Captain Hawke was still alive or after she married Captain Hill. There are no initials on it. I don't know if there's a way to date this. Camelias bloom in the winter in South Carolina. She wouldn't have spent that many holidays there with Captain Hawke. It will be interesting to go back and match when she moved into the home and left it," Angie said.

Two hours later, Angie and Matt were back on the highway.

Matt broke his silence. "I'm glad we found it. It only reinforces the story I have in mind of what happened. However, I'm not willing to talk about it further presently. What is on my mind is finding the lovely little hotel we arranged for tonight and taking a hot bath to warm my body. Then I want to snuggle closely for heat conservation for the rest of the evening."

"I like that plan a lot. By tomorrow night, we will be back in our warm bed. Sam and Bella will be part of a growing family again."

Matt sighed with a frown. "You've been holding secrets. Not Bella! I like our cute little bunny. But I can't take several bunny bundles at once. We will have to adopt out. I'm not negotiating."

"It's not Bella," Angie whispered.

"Sam's a boy dog, Angie, and I've had taken care of consequences of unexpected cohabitation beyond my control." When he got no response, Matt looked at Angie and realized she had a stoic expression. "Stupid husband, huh? You're not talking about four-legged housemates, are you? You're talking about the two of us?"

Angie smiled, nodding "affirmatively."

"Are you sure?"

"Pretty sure," Angie responded.

"Wow! That is big news. It's terrific news! I want to process what you are saying. Give me a moment here," Matt said. He had an enormous smile on his face. Please accept my apologies and I want to rephrase what I said earlier. I want more of these bundles of joy. Pink, yellow, green, or blue, I don't care. I will love them all the same. If there are two or pink, I will give them to you after the age of eleven until the age of twenty-one because I'm not so sure about those teenage years. They become aliens with all that crying and boyfriend stuff. You would be a much better parent during that period of their lives."

"Oh, that's sweet of you, thanks." Angie replied.

In the next few hours, Matt and his wife would close the window of the visit to her family and the side trips made to explore the family connections further. The thought of returning to their home on the island was welcoming. There was much to do and prepare for when they returned, and both were excited to start the next chapter but reluctant to leave the honeymoon period of their lives.

Chapter 24

THE FOUR WEEKS between Thanksgiving and Christmas were a blur. Matt and Angie were working hard on their jobs to finish so they could enjoy the holiday with the Fitz family and company. That meant anyone who showed up at their door on Christmas Eve was welcome. Matt's Christmas present of a baby grand piano showed up at 8:00 AM on December 24th. He was happy he no longer had to explain why he wanted to move the leather recliner into the extra bedroom.

Angie had to be sneakier. She had to wait until Matt left the house for Christmas Eve for Angie to call Lauren and Carl to bring the crate over with the lift. She had fibbed about what she was doing in his home office, making measurements. Now he would understand. By the time he returned, the display case was in the open in his office with all in place, with the light toggle placed on soft lighting to add a glow. The other gift she would save for a private moment, perhaps at midnight or first thing when he woke.

The house was buzzing with excitement as people came by. It was an open house vibe for Christmas Eve. Next year would be different when the baby arrived. Matt's parents pulled into the drive and resupplied the cookie tray and finger foods that Matt's mother was so good at. They found their room for the night decorated with a tree and presents underneath. Since Matt was the only child, he loved to spoil his parents now as they've grown older with the touches of comfort and home. Matt's parents loved to entertain and enjoyed the merriment of Matt's and Angie's friends passing by to enjoy the season. By 9:00 PM, calm was returning to the household once again. Trash was removed, soft music was played on the piano by Mr. Fitz, and all were ready to sit in front of the fireplace and relax.

"I love your playing," Angie said to Matt's father.

"Well, thank you. I don't play the one we have much. The temptation of playing this baby grand was too much. I hope you don't mind."

"You blessed us this evening with your music," Matt said.

"Your mother and I used to love music when we were younger, all kinds."

"Dad don't lie. There was some music I would play that you hated."

"Well, that's true, son, but I let you play that screeching stuff if I couldn't hear it in the library. I let you pick your poison. I would pick which battle to fight with a teenage boy with a stubborn streak."

"Mom, is that what you thought while I grew up?" Matt teased.

"Oh no! My goals were not as lofty as your father's. I just wanted to love everybody under our roof. That was my only plan in life, and I've worked hard to make that happen. I've never regretted wearing my fighting clothes to love my family."

"I watched you do laundry, Mom. There wasn't anything in the washer but T-shirts, jeans, and Dad's boxer shorts. That doesn't sound like a soldier's uniform to me."

"You're right, son. I, like you, was on the special forces team and needed top-secret items to keep you and your father to complete my mission. The things you didn't see were my secret weapons. For you, it was the navy power suit I wore to the principal's office each time I was called in to address some foolish thing you did. For your father, we'll say some things were kept in the restricted access category."

Matt laughed will all the others in the room. "I should know better than to mess with my mother after all these years. She'll have the last word every time."

"That's right!" Mrs. Fitz added.

The evening ended after midnight, after a toast and a few sips of champagne. Angie was quick to sneak a ginger ale in her glass, hiding her pregnancy until the packages were unwrapped in the morning, just like children by the tree.

At 7:00 AM, Christmas was official at the Fitz home by the beach. It started with a planned group activity down on the beach.

However, Matt's mother and dad preferred the bikes waiting for them on the front porch when they went outside to make their way out to the path. And so, they zoomed ahead like they were young again, still in their dating years and enjoying each other's companionship.

Matt and Angie followed behind, not jogging this morning. Instead, the pace was a comfortable stroll, which included Sam. The family pet pranced in the sand and dabbed his paws in the water occasionally as the tide expanded its reach closer toward the dunes on each new wave.

Matt responded. "I like Christmas. The baby will be here next year, and I'll love that too."

"I'm glad that you feel that way. Hey, look! There are a couple of dolphins out there. Right there!"

Matt turned to where Angie was pointing.

"Yes, I see them." He turned his face back to Angie and saw her profile as she was still staring towards the sea, her hair strands blowing in the wind. The sun cast a glowing shine on her skin, creamy white, dewy, and smooth. She was a vision of a goddess. His gaze drifted down her neck to the opening of her crimson-colored warm-up jacket. Before his eyes could drift lower, they stopped at the area in the center of her chest just below the collar bones. "Angie, what are you wearing?" Matt's voice was heard just above a whisper.

Angie turned toward her husband. "Is this what you've been looking for?" She made no further movement but saw her husband's eyes fixed on her open neckline.

"Where did you find it?" Matt asked incredulously.

"You've had it all along, at least longer than you've known me," Angie responded.

"Where?"

"Before I answer that question, tell me where you've looked for it," Angie replied.

"Everywhere!" Matt responded. "No, it's been since my injury. I had an image. I wasn't sure if the necklace even existed. The image was of someone with the chain pulling me out of consciousness. I never told you because I wasn't sure of what had happened. I just wanted to know if it was real."

"Who did you see?" Angie asked.

Matt touched Angie's cheek. "I saw Naya, and she was pulling me one way. Then, I saw someone else with the necklace pulling me out of the hole of darkness. It may have been the face of someone I didn't know, but now I realize it was you. You pulled me out of that black hole."

"I won't deny that my prayers for protection were there. But what you may have seen was not me alone. I wouldn't have found you alone. I would have been lost. You wouldn't have seen me unless you were looking in the right direction," Angie responded. "I wasn't sure it was real."

"Yes, it was real," Angie said.

Matt reached for Angie's hand and walked again along the shore. "Dr. Santoro, who is researching a different topic, shared with me some new information before we left for Thanksgiving. The sketches we saw in that museum proved it had existed. I hadn't hallucinated on the island. When Naya died, I lost faith that love still existed. All that love my parents gave me was blocked out by the darkness that consumed me."

Angie reached up, removed the necklace, and put it in his hand. "I found this hidden in the frame of the captain's portrait. I suspect it was given to him when she was on that ship crossing the Atlantic for protection and remembrance. He still went by the name of Luke Shaw—first mate on the ship from Londonderry to Philadelphia. The older sketch we saw in Pennsylvania when she was older was done at Christmas of 1783 after the British left the city of Charleston. She still owned the home in Charleston. The British militia protected her property because she was a widow of a British officer. At least the militia did. The naval bombardment had no favorites, but the home was off the harbor, so it was a little more protected. Kitty rented the home to an officer and his wife, who she had made friends with while she was married. She and her parents went to England for a short time to take care of some financial arrangements, as her husband was a British citizen. By the time she returned to Charleston in 1783, she was already married to Captain Thomas Hill. CH did the sketching but with the same handwriting as LS. I suspect the captain let his guard down momentarily as he signed it for her. Typically, Captain Hill was more careful with matching handwriting before September 1777 and after. Before they died, it must have been placed in a compartment on the frame. Perhaps that was done by Mr. Fitz, who would have had a closer relationship with both parties. He would have known Captain Hill's wishes and the will's contents. Mr. Fitz grew up as a successful young man in mining, railroad, and later oil. That Mr. Fitz was the ancestor of the present, Matt Fitz, I believe."

"I married a brilliant and beautiful woman. That took some research." Matt replied.

"It did indeed!" Angie smiled. "I wanted to know who I was going to marry." Angie teased.

"All that, and you still chose me. How did I deserve to make the Christmas list this year?" Matt said as he kissed her on the cheek. "Thank you for this extraordinary Christmas present. I will always cherish it." Matt said.

"No, you got it all wrong! You didn't make the stocking list this year! Your presents are the consolation prize. Just think about what you missed. Maybe next year?" Angie teased.

"Oh, I can't wait for next year's holiday then! I'll show you what a good guy I can be."

About the Author

D.L. Barnes is a pen name for the author who lives near Atlanta, Georgia. The Coastal Saga Series was created from the author's love of the natural beauty of the Carolina and Georgia coasts.

www.ingramcontent.com/pod-product-compliance
Lightning Source LLC
Chambersburg PA
CBHW030607310726
48979CB00003B/610

* 9 7 9 8 2 1 8 2 2 2 2 3 9 *